Apr 2015

Also by Jeffrey Rotter
The Unknown Knowns

THE ONLY WORDS THAT ARE
WORTH REMEMBERING

THE ONLY WORDS THAT ARE WORTH REMEMBERING

A   NOVEL

JEFFREY ROTTER

METROPOLITAN BOOKS
HENRY HOLT AND COMPANY
NEW YORK

Metropolitan Books
Henry Holt and Company, LLC
Publishers since 1866
175 Fifth Avenue
New York, New York 10010
www.henryholt.com

Metropolitan Books® and ⅿ® are registered trademarks
of Henry Holt and Company, LLC.

Library of Congress Cataloging-in-Publication Data

Rotter, Jeffrey.
The only words that are worth remembering : a novel / Jeffrey Rotter.—First edition.
    pages ; cm
    ISBN 978-1-62779-152-6 (hardcover)—ISBN 978-1-62779-153-3 (electronic book)
I. Title.
PS3618.O8693O55 2015
813'.6—dc23   2014028456

Henry Holt books are available for special promotions and premiums. For details contact:
Director, Special Markets.

First Edition 2015
Designed by Meryl Sussman Levavi
Printed in the United States of America

1 2 3 4 5 6 7 8 9 10

For my family

THE ONLY WORDS THAT ARE
WORTH REMEMBERING

1.

My father always had either too much gentleness or too much fight. But after he started cracking eggs at Airplane Food, Pop entered a kindly spell that looked to be permanent. Umma said he had gone too decent to ever switch back to bad again. He did not hit or holler nor break any man's two legs for telling him he couldn't pitch a tent on private property. He did not seem capable of murdering someone who cheated him out of a drink.

I couldn't have been more pleased with his change of temperament, but my twin brother thought Pop now cared too much. He'd gone soft, said Faron, and could not earn a boy's respect behaving as he did.

On the rare occasion when they found an embro inside one of those eggs, the rest of the crackers at Airplane Food would not hesitate to dump it in the scramble vat with the rest. But not Pop. He told Umma it hurt his chest to look upon those pitiful creatures, to hold one in his latex-gloved hands till its visible blue heart expired. They were about to become something, he said, and to fling them into the vat was a wretched insult to chicken life.

The customer had more gastromical complaints. The sort that flies on airplanes has nothing better to gripe about than pinfeathers in their breakfast platters. To discourage the crackers from dumping embros in the scramble, management made a game of it. Whoever collected the most by the end of a working week could take home a liter of Haven Dark rum. Pop wanted so badly to win this contest, because he'd done time in the Cuba Pens chopping sugarcane for the Bosom rum concern. If he could get a liter free of charge, it would feel like a restitution.

Contest or no, Pop remained vigilant. He watched what went in the vat, and what came out the bottom. Never once did he expectorate in the vicinity of the scramble. He kept a consistent stir with the big plexiglas paddle. And Pop made himself well worth the management's dollar. Careful as he was, he could crack a gross in fifteen minutes, which put him squarely in the top five.

Winning that game of embros was what did Pop in, and it set in miserable motion the whole starry trajectory of the Van Zandt family.

* * *

It was Meet Your Future Day at Airplane Food, a Friday. Offspring of employs had the privilege of laboring alongside their parents, seeing how the world worked. We shared Pop's cracking station, on a gangway about ten feet above the vat. I followed his example; not a speck of shell landed in the scramble. If Faron dropped an egg on the floor, he did not hesitate to kick it in whole.

We were both of us bully proud of our father. He had won the embro tally that week. He showed us the bucket of baby chicks that had been used to verify the count, and he displayed his jug of Haven Dark atop an egg crate for all the other crackers to envy.

Two hours till quitting time and we were looking forward to a night of rum and song on our bunks in the Airplane Food dormitory. I made Pop promise he'd bust out the Roland AX. I wasn't supposed to know that Umma had been saving a Canaday goose for roasting, but I did.

Then along comes a fellow across the gangway to Pop's crack station. I Murder was his name, though I am sure the irony was lost on him at the end. He was not too large and none too nice. The little thug pushed his chest against big Pop's gut and started into the bully talk.

"I will have it," said I Murder, by which he meant the rum. He spoke in a Caribeen brogue.

Now this man was exactly what his name declared: homicidal. If he hadn't been born and raised in the Cuba Pens, he would have landed there anyway. Both his parents had been Water Bombers, people of conviction, self-educated and violent. His grandparents were worse. Commies of the old breed. Folks like them were the reason Consolidated War & Jail partnered up with Dutch Bosom to turn the whole island of Cuba into a jailhouse and distillery. Easier to lock down the reds and runners where they lived.

I Murder was a boy when his mama died. After his pa stopped participating in life, he was raised by turnkeys, including an old lady whose job it was to shoot bats. Her name was Cruz and she was just as good a shot with human targets.

By the time Pop got hired at Airplane Food, I Murder ran his own private Gunt from the factory break room, a fiefdom of eggs of which he was the baby chief, unquestioned and plenty rich. He took home a tub of leftover scrambles each night to sell in the Colatown favelers. People said he owned a car. If it was Pop's rum he wanted, it was rum he would get.

Unfortunately I Murder's status meant nothing to Pop. And here is where we get to my father's condition. He could be so decent and kind that you'd be forgiven for thinking Pop could be pushed around. He offered to everyone a soft smile, a bashful hello, a musical greeting card if it was your birthday. But a point would come, dictated by the moon or hormones or your own bad luck, when he would switch. And then the very large man I came from, the man with scarred hands and red braids down his strong back, would make you pay whatever price it was he thought you owed. And near everybody was in arrears.

Faron saw it before I did: the light go dim in Pop's eye. He heard the troubling moan escape his big wax lips. My brother knew I was the kind of fairy-boy that gets crushed between powerful men, so he did his best to protect me. He hurried me down the steps to a lower landing, at eye level with the vat.

I could barely breathe for Faron's weight on top of me and the odor of bulk-made breakfast. Up through the steel grid of catwalks we watched the two men prepare to fight.

Faron told me later that he felt sorry for that Cuban runt, though I doubt his sincerity. I remember the grin on my brother's face, the pride that lit up his eyes. His Pop was back. His father: the bad one.

I took Pop's old wallet from my back pocket and gave it a good chew. This was a habit of mine when circumstances spun beyond my control, which was most always. My brother's weight was on me so hard, the steel grid cut a design on my calf. But this was no time to complain. It would have been a good time to warn I Murder, though, and I wish I had been bold enough to do so. Pop was fixing to end that man's life if he didn't back away from the crack station and apologize.

"That rum," said I Murder, "is mine."

The muscles of our old man's face went slack like a sail. He would not be told what was or wasn't his. Pop put down his unbroken eggs—he cracked them in pairs. He returned them so gently to the foam cradle, as if he had laid them himself.

"I won that jug fair," he said. I bit the wallet somewhat harder, feeling for the consolation of old toothmarks. Pop showed him the bucket: "Sixteen embros. Mr. Destin counted."

I know that Pop did not want to switch at that moment. After all, this was Meet Your Future Day. His boys were watching, learning by example, and he'd sworn to Umma that he would never give them reason to send him back to the Pens again. But when those malicious juices welled up in his tubes, it was like indigestion of a moral order.

Years later, when I shot fink in my arm behind a Caroline sand dune or nodded off in the throne room of Castle Kintek, I understood what Pop meant when he said trying to be good was like standing in heavy surf. The waves pour in and chew the sand around your feet till you're balanced on two hard points. Then comes the big breaker, and no man, even one as strong as Pop, can stand his ground.

I Murder did not care about Pop's victory in the embro contest. He cared nothing for the rum. He only despised fairness and would do what he could to corrupt it. The Cuban reached for the jug like it had always been his. That was the last justice the little bully ever tried to reverse.

Ten feet below them a four-hundred-gallon vat gasped and gagged—white, yellow, it burped yolk into the propane-sweetened air. The opening was wide as a water tower. A ring of gas jets underneath made an awful hiss. At intervals a valve on the bottom spurted cooked egg onto cardboard platters. Triangles of toast shuffled down a second conveyor belt. Each tray got two, sprayed with oleo, before it passed through the heat-sealer and landed on a palette to be shipped to the world's airports.

Pop touched the soft patch of his own throat, like he was a Jesus Lover blessing himself, but he was in fact rehearsing. Then he found I Murder's neck and lifted the man off the gangway. Pop said it again: that rum was nobody's except his.

The little man carried a blade, as a character like that often does. I watched from below as he slipped it into Pop's ribs like he was opening the mail. To so immense a body, that shiv meant nothing, but the shock of it made Pop's switch complete. He swung out over the vat still holding the smaller man, so that I Murder's flipper-flops clapped right by my head. I remember worrying: what if he drops a shoe in the scramble? I Murder clawed at Pop's eyes, but he didn't have the reach. Pop held him stiff-armed, steady as a crane and about as caring when it drops a load of bricks.

The dagger stuck in Pop's rib cage after I Murder fell away. When he hit the scramble, hot egg splashed across my face. It slopped over the sides of the vat and blue flame followed it up, filling the air with sulfur. We could see too clearly a man trying to swim in boiling paste. He tested one stroke then another but didn't swim well or for long. Already his flesh was puffing up. The blisters popped and peeled away with each turn of the paddle. Fresh blisters took their place.

Pop didn't see the two guards cross the gangway. He shut his eyes and rocked from heel to heel hugging that bucket of embros like it was a baby. A voice on the floor shouted *switch it off, switch it off.* The propane jets went quiet. Somebody propped a ladder against the side of the vat. I bit a hole clear through Pop's wallet.

The man's organs were roasting inside him now. A fork would have slipped easily into his thigh. Gore jetted from his neck to thicken in the heat. Rusty knobs, blood sausage. Some faces you will recall your whole life. I have seen a few of them, silent begging at the end. I Murder's mouth made a line. It parted as if to speak. His lips drew back. I believe the muscles were contracting as they cooked. His teeth were silver.

Pop's boots thundered overhead as they dragged him down the steps. I heard him keen like a dray horse. He was a beast bred for strength and compliance who now strained at the bridle. I looked back to see a woman haul I Murder's body out with a hook. He was the ham in the omelet, precisely that significant and exactly that dead.

The gas ring was relit. The valve resumed its pattern, opening and closing like a heart. It could release a thousand servings of egg every hour. Somewhere, early the next morning, a jet would skim under the Night Glass, beneath our fading stars. A passenger would gaze out the window without admiring the view. Stars are flaws in the globe of the sky. He would know this to be true and would only pity the night for its imperfections. "Yes," he would say, in answer to the flight attendant, "the eggs are just fine, thanks. But I could use another sugar for my tea."

In all the confusion nobody took notice of me and Faron. My brother grabbed the rum and back to the dorms we walked all alone. It was understood that he would break the news to Umma. Understood because I could not stop shaking to speak. Pop would spend the night in a holding cell down in Georgietown. Next morning they would chain his legs to the rail of a gunboat and float him back to the Cuba Pens. So began our sorrow.

* * *

Now, ten years on, I am left with the solitude. This evening First Light came to the Paranal Observatory. The only remaining telescope on Earth opened her single mirrored eye, and after three blind centuries she found the stars unmoved by human history.

At last the old light from distant galaxies drips down the eight-meter barrel, scarcely enough to feed the glow of a computer screen and illuminate the salvaged legal pad on which I write this story, this explanation and apology, to you, dear daughter.

One day, Little Sylvia, when you are older, you will resent me for what I have taken from you. When you were a baby I carried you by train and by bus, away from the broken world up north so that you might hide here on a mountaintop in the Chilly desert—far from anywhere but close to the stars. Little Sylvia, when you are old enough, I hope you will read this and I hope you will understand why your father did what he did.

As you sweat and breathe in a sleepsack on the couch behind me, I write this down so that you will know: I gave you solitude, sweet daughter, so that you will never be lonely.

No one should be as lonely as Umma was after they took Pop away.

2.

FOR KILLING I MURDER, POP RECEIVED A LONG STRETCH in the Cuba Pens, but only if he behaved himself. If he promised to be quiet and polite, he could labor in the sugarcane fields till malaria, heat, tube poisoning, or some better thug laid him out.

Though he had been taken far away from us, my mother believed in the propagating nature of love. Love as a particle and a wave. She was descended from Jesus Lovers and carried with her many of their magical ideas. Love, she said, bridged distances the human eye could not, which sounds like nonsense until you need it to be true. But even love had its limits, so she moved us as close to the Cuba Pens as was legally possible.

The Gables is a township up the Dixie Hiway from Old Miamy. To the north is Hiya City, a geriatric stronghold. Directly south are the Miamy Ruins, which were a big tourist draw and a Bosom Industries asset. The Gables was the farthest south a free person could live, the bottom of the unincarcerated world, and approximately three hundred miles north of Pop's prison cell.

The night we moved into Residential Tower C, Umma stood by the south-facing window while me and Faron unpacked our duffel bags. She remained there till it went dark, head cocked like she was listening. After a while her body went rigid. Those drumstick shoulders hitched up in their puff sleeves, and she made a noise I had never heard her make before. I believe my mother was moaning, and not from grief. Faron asked did she need a glass of water. I asked did she need a tissue. Umma told us be quiet; she was feeling him.

Pop's love was not a vibration or a breeze or a glow, she said. It was like ordnance. With a blast radius as wide as the Caribeen. From his cell down in the Cuba Pens, she could feel him go *thud, thud, thud*. Umma called that love, but I know now that Pop was punching the walls of his cell.

The Gables was a step up from sharecropper tents and factory dorms. I hear it's all faveler now, but in my boyhood the tower blocks were respectable living. Our junior-plus one-bedroom was on the top floor. Us boys thought it was a penthouse. Galvanized steel door, en suite kitchen, sit-down toilet right across the hall. The carpets were soft and beige, beige walls and beige window treatments—the décor blended so seamlessly with the Floriday summer sky that our home seemed to expand out into the greater world. Our bunks were hinged to the living room wall. I called top on account of my claustrophobia, but I usually woke up on the couch beside Umma.

The only drawback to tower living was the eleven flights we had to climb up and down each day. If you had pocket change you could afford the elevator. The steps cost you more anyway. The Stairdwellers shook you down hard, and if your pockets were empty they made sure teeth fell out instead. I wouldn't risk it without Faron. He was my muscle.

Umma was my warmth. I would like to say love, but mostly she saved that for Pop. She was a wiry woman but hot, like the coils of an electric stove. In those days after our father went to Cuba, Umma did not embrace us; she coiled around us until our skin began to burn.

She meant to make a better life for me and Faron so she enrolled at the Old Miamy School for Drugs and Doctors. She'd always been crack at sewing up Faron's playground wounds. She could read decent well, and the clinics were so hard up for physicians they would take anyone. I believe there was also a measure of pity in their decision to accept her, though no serious person would admit to such an outmoded senti-ment. Umma chose obeegy, making babies.

When she did her rounds at the babying clinic, Umma wore a calico dress some nurse had left behind in the lockers. It was a few sizes too large, and the gathered front pockets were always weighed down with stray objects she'd collected throughout the day. This was her idea of housekeeping. When she went to sleep I would go through them looking for my books, pencils, or underpants.

One night, when we'd been living in the Gables about four or five months, I dug through her pockets in search of Pop's wallet. Instead, I found a canvas bundle the size of a grande burrito. The inside was carefully stitched with little flaps that contained what appeared to be medical supplies—syringes, needles, brown tinctures in plastic bags. A small square of paper fell out and I picked it up. In a cautious, cramped hand—not my mother's—someone had written:

YOU DONT HAVE TO.

I have always been good at waiting. I was born to keep vigil. Umma's shifts at the clinic ran till midnight six days a week. When the red digits of the oven clock showed twelve I would climb onto my bunk and survey the elevated stretch of Dixie Hiway. It ran so close to our tenement that you could leap across from a stairwell window on the third floor. And it was so empty, I had no trouble picking out my mother's frail shadow as she walked the hiway home. Good Samaritans made bonfires of cottonwood and scrub pine to scare away coyotes and light the way. If you stayed clear of the median you were safe enough, but still I worried.

It was always much past midnight when Umma's calico dress finally appeared on the firelit roadway. She would look up and wave before vanishing around the side of our building. Faron always met her in the lobby to keep her safe from the Stairdwellers. They were a special sort of edgy after midnight, but so was Faron. He got himself stabbed in the arm once with a coat hanger.

Sometimes Umma liked to stop at the bonfires to comfort herself with her fellow commuters, and that comfort might stretch on for hours. Some nights I'd nod off before she made it home. My eyes would swim out over the Dixie Hiway and the shadows that pressed in around its bonfires, over the ruins of Old Miamy all pink and lit up for the nighttime tourists. I'd wake up smelling wood smoke and know our mother had come home. She would bind me up in the hot wires of her arms. I would burn in the folds of her calico and fall asleep.

* * *

Me and Faron did our Vocationals in Mining. Your uncle took to the dirt like a regulation earthworm. He could crawl on his belly down seepholes with no clue where he might emerge. The earth would close around him, he said, like a big mineral hug. It made him feel like a part of something.

Me, I felt like dinner down there. Stepping into a mineshaft was like feeding myself to a giant. Tight spaces, thin air, total darkness: what separated mining from the grave was a paycheck, and you earned almost as much dead.

As the months wore on and I missed Pop more and more, I started playing hooky from Vocationals to ride the tour bus through the Old Miamy Ruins. I liked the sun and wind and the smell of lotion. The tour was gratis because the Bosom Chiefs considered those ruins a history lesson. I learned by heart the haunting names of Old Miamy's landmarks. Civil Center, Bass, Arse, Jungle Island. Before long I could parrot back the whole boilerplate script.

Whenever a tourist asked me to take her picture in front of the Four Seasons, I felt it my duty to oblige. Hundreds of people had contributed to that shell of a building; thousands had enjoyed its ice machines, imported bedclothes, and heated lap pool. I owed it to them to tell their story. Their dissolution held promise for us as a society. It is a comfort to know how swiftly and thoroughly a civilization can crumble when nobody wants it anymore.

The highlight of every Miamy tour was Pork & Beans. This was a gated housing compound built by the famed Commie Gunt called Roserfelt. He was a Chief in his own way, stinky rich and hitched up to the finest families, but old Roserfelt had a deviant attachment to the poor. It may have been sexual. He wanted to see them pampered and put up like sultans, so he gave them Pork & Beans. He gave them police and water at no extra charge. Men addicted to drugs and women hooked on pregnancy got free sirloin and sedans and potable water. Swimming pools, in-unit toilets, a doctor that made house calls in a hi-tech van: Pork & Beans was paradise for do-nothings. I paid special attention to getting this part of the tour just right and would practice it every chance I got.

Pop had always been one to encourage my hobbies; he would have listened patiently to my Pork & Beans speech, clapped me on the back, and narrowed his earnest eyes. "You will amount to something, boy."

But in Pop's absence Faron was in charge. That we were twins and should have been equals made no difference. (Umma told us after Faron was born it took me a full hour to work my way out of her tubes.) My brother decided I should not entertain any dreams as lofty as Old Miamy tour guide. He said mining was a safe bet for both of us.

One morning in late summer, after Umma went to the clinic and before we were to report for Vocationals, I made the mistake of practicing Pork & Beans on Faron. He stood behind the kitchen bar making steam patterns on the laminate with his toast. I hung my legs over the edge of the top bunk and started in.

As I laid bare the terrible history of the Pork & Beans housing complex, I could sense my brother's rising irritation. He ground his toast to dust on the counter. When I reached the end of my speech—"The tower blocks were painted a cheery pink to match the flamingo, a narcissistic bird that eats garbage"—he leaned forward and blew a cloud of crumbs across the living room.

He stalked over and kicked his lower bunk flush against the wall. Though I didn't get it at the time, the implication was that I needed to be crushed a little myself. Faron always meant well. He was my protector, especially when it came to disappointment.

"You want to be a tour guide so bad?" he said. "Get down."

I followed him into the stairwell, awed by his tone. He was our man of action and I loved him dearly, even when he went too far. Only one Stairdweller dared to give us trouble. She was a ropy gal in a handcrafted shirt made out of Fatty Meats take-out bags. She wagged a sharpened prybar and told us to open our rucksacks. I offered her a sandwich but before she could take it Faron punched her in the neck. The girl hacked so hard I thought she might die, but then she coughed up something and spat at me.

The next landing was where the Stairdwellers kept rabbits. As I often did, I stopped to poke a finger in the hutch, but it wasn't a bunny that sniffed me. It was a boy. Dry blood colored his mouth. The surviving rabbits huddled in a back corner, ears down. Their eyes were asking for help, same as the boy that had eaten one of their kin. "Don't dwell on it," said Faron, advice he gave me often, though it never stuck.

At the third floor we hopped over the windowsill and onto the overpass. We took the Dixie Hiway till we reached the deco gate of the Ruins. A fat boy with cornrows tried to shake us down for five hundred dollars each, but he didn't force the issue. Soon as Faron touched his shoulder, we were let inside free of charge.

While we waited at the bus kiosk, my brother's attitude softened. He sprung for sno-cones. I got grape and though the syrup tasted like a tin spoon, I sucked the ice till it turned brittle and white.

The bus, when it came, was done up like an old-time trolley. The paint job was flamingo pink. Said FLAMINGO FLYER on both sides.

"Goddamn 'mingos," said Faron. He was racist about birds. Meaning his contempt for birds was disordered and based on ignorance. I thought there were good species and bad. Even turkey vultures have their virtues if you are looking for a dead body.

I recognized the bus driver. Ross Carnation was one of my favorite guides. He was a star because he put a little music in his voice, like he was singing quietly to the passengers. He sang about arrogance, about collapse and decay, without cruelty. Ross lived a few floors below us in Tower C, and was a revival dancer of some note. Saturday nights he'd gather in the courtyard with a bunch of guys to dance to trad music like Miamy bass and salser. Sometimes they put on a floor show for the whole Gables, which was a pleasure to attend. I always thought Pop would have liked to sit in with his Roland AX and make them dance to some of those gloomy sweet songs from his Texas forebear, but he never got the chance.

We climbed on through the back of the bus like I always did. I never wanted to be a nuisance. But Faron pushed his way to the front and I followed through a gauntlet of varicose knees. Thursdays was for geriatrics, come down in their Vansters from Hiya City.

Ross reached for the mic to announce our next stop. It would be the zoo, one of my favorites. Faron was quicker than the dancer. He snagged the handset and passed it to me. "Do your thing, brother," he said. "If you want it so bad." Ross gave me a pointy look and said something that had no trace of music in it.

I could have made the announcement easy; I knew all my lines, but why make trouble? Ross was all right; he could dance.

"Start talking," said Faron.

The geriatrics were getting impatient, too. It started up like gas, a rumble in the springs of their seats. The Hiya City crowd came here on a weekly basis. They were old and had no trouble doing the same thing over and over again. At the ends of their lives they had a vested interest in maintaining the status quo. Patterns were life itself to them. When a pattern changed, they were forced to consider broader shifts in being.

"I'm dying," somebody moaned. "Just do the god-durned speech!" She was joined by several of her peers: "Let's hear some talking points!" an old frog hollered. A girly voice kept saying, "Make it talk, make it talk, make it talk."

Ross grabbed at the mic, but Faron intervened. He yanked open Ross's waistband and dropped the sno-cone inside his gym shorts. Ross hopped into the well shaking ice out of his crotch like a snow turd. Faron yanked the lever that made the door open, and we watched Ross bounce off toward the front gate.

"Oh man," I said. "He's going to tell."

Faron sucked his teeth and swung into the driver's seat. "This is your big shot," he said. "If you want to be a tour guide so damn bad, brother, start talking and see how much you like it."

I don't know how I felt, only that I didn't want to be a tour guide quite so badly anymore. If Faron was trying to kill my dream, it was working. I wanted to get off that bus, bolt down the Dixie Hiway, and never come back. I wanted to hide in the rabbit hutch with that bloody-mouth boy. But Faron was looking at me and so were the old people.

"Next we come to the place the ancient Floridayans called Zoo Miamy," I began, too quietly. Soon, though, the words began to flow, and despite my fear I could not shut up. "It is widely known that Gunts and their subjects were Christian animists who elevated the lower species to the respect level of gods. They built temples in their honor, fed them gourmet. Animals that would eat you if you gave them a fork and knife the Gunts coddled like Chiefs."

We paused under the ruined signage, rebar and clods of cement that hardly formed the word *Zoo*.

"Beyond this gate," I continued, "citizens would pay a tithe to gigantic rats, long-neck horses in pokey-dots, and virus monkeys. Excited with sugar drinks, children gave in to the rapturous worship of beasts." It was a hell of a speech, and today I can't believe I delivered it so straight.

I praised the Chiefs, in whose wisdom the facility was shut down and all the useless species exterminated for the security of mankind. "Many of these creatures would appear fantastical to us today. Great big kitties they painted like fire, a fake man in an orange fringe jacket who lived in a tree. They called him the Orange Tan. . . ."

This was as much of the script as I could manage before the bus surged forward and I landed in a bony grandpa lap. At the bleat of a siren I looked back to see that we were being pursued by an enforcement sedan.

Tour buses were forbidden entry into the zoo proper. Officially it was because the footpaths were too narrow for vehicular traffic. But the real reason, I had been told, was the presence of certain dangerous species that had survived these many years since the park's closing. They had thrived in a state of wildness for centuries, growing more resentful of their former captors with each generation. If the Chiefs had believed in

Darwin, they might have called it natural selection, the evolution of spite.

But Faron did not know this. Or perhaps he did and was figuring the cops would never follow us into so dangerous a place. We crashed through a cyclone fence, bouncing around pylons and derelict ticket booths. Just inside the gates stood a pack of flamingoes. The flamingo is not a flightless bird, only unmotivated. Faron flipped on the wipers to clear away the blood and feathers, just in time to reveal a gift shop directly in our path. To the left lay a broad marsh that must have been artificial when it was built but was now very real. Faron swung hard to the right, landing the front wheels in a moat.

Two squad cars braked behind us and a third piled into our rear bumper. Our more ambulatory passengers made for the back door, but there was no time to escape. After much cursing Faron found reverse. He backed onto the footpath in a spray of gravel. There was only one way to turn. We hit the marsh at a high rate of speed, but it wasn't fast enough to carry us across. The bus mired in about two feet of water and the engine died.

Back on the path the cops killed their sirens like it was mission accomplished, suspects apprehended, roger that. I heard nothing but the chatter of cranes and car doors opening. Two officers, pistols drawn, approached the edge of the marsh. We were, I believed at that moment, done for. But then the cops turned and ran back to their squad car. From the rear of the bus I watched two gators slither onto the shoal. I checked the side windows. A long bull swam underneath us and emerged with a hiss on the other side.

Cops were one thing. We had survived their interventions before, but I was ill prepared for gators. However, they proved to be a blessing. The engine turned over, and Faron stomped the gas. The wheels caught and the bus bolted up onto the far bank. Mud must have flooded the brake drums because there was no stopping us. Dead ahead stood a tremendous column of bark, a tree so big, so fleshy, it looked like the leg of an out-of-shape giant. We struck it head-on. I watched Faron float through the shattering windshield and slam against the tree before I was buried under a pig pile of old folks. Nobody moved, though there was much groaning and the odor of ruptured bladder bags.

The girly voice said, "Pee-ew!"

I elbowed myself free and crawled over the dashboard to save my brother.

In the mangrove I found him, insensible but more or less intact. I looked him over. One foot was turned perpendicular to the other. He appeared to be growing a second forehead on his first one. I got under one arm and tried to help him across the savanna. Not an easy task; Faron was all muscle and half awake. I didn't have time to check on the geriatrics piled up inside the bus, but they had the look about them of a mass grave.

Across the marsh two cops with shotguns pumped rounds into the gators. The beasts did not go down easy. They opened their jaws like they could eat the shells.

The nearest hidey-hole was a low silo of concrete. I found an opening overhung with kudzu and pushed Faron inside. The door was marked with a skirted hieroglyph: the ancient symbol for ladies. I dragged my brother inside the bathroom. Sunlight bore down through the roof. It gleamed across a row of basins loaded with shit. Animals are basically decent but they do not know better than to take their dumps in the sink. It may be true what Smart Man Tolemy said, that plumbing is the divide between man and beasts. But that fool said a lot of things.

I stuck two fingers in the knob hole and pulled the door tight behind us. Faron blacked out with his head in a basin of white scat. I cleared a patch on the counter and settled my brother atop it. There were leaves in his hair and crap on his nose. His pupils kept trying to size up the light. Cold scum covered his face. His head lolled against the backsplash and he kept saying the word *ponies* with great emphasis, like he meant something by it. If we hoped to get out of this shithouse I needed my brother at least semi-functional. Maybe, I thought, a splash of water would revive him. When I turned the tap, a centipede spooled out of the faucet.

Kneeling down, I inspected his ankle. Faron's foot was so swollen that the straps of his flipper-flop trussed it up like a pork roast. I pried away the foam sole and just held his leg to my chest. Maybe I could will it to repair. Maybe I had Umma's touch. We only had to reach the clinic, find her. Umma would know what to do. I found the wallet in my back pocket and gnawed on it, listening to Faron breathe.

His ragged breath seemed to echo through the lavatory. From somewhere in the room I heard a congested sort of panting, a snuffling laugh. I thought: we are not alone. I thought: some joker is making fun of my brother.

This old bathroom had two narrow stalls for the able and one wide for cripples, who were rewarded for their inadequacies in those days with roomier commodes. The breathing came from behind that handicap door.

I saw movement in the gap above the floor. A baggy nose, shining with snot, appeared and then withdrew. The door banged open to reveal a specimen of unprecedented ugliness. It was pig-based, but beyond that I can say little more. Its head was black and burred all over like a charred cactus. Tusks curled up in a handlebar mustache of villainy. The tail stood upright, and Cactus Pig charged.

Its hooves slid across the tiles. I ducked under the sink to make a shield of Faron's shins. Cactus Pig stopped, sniffed us, put its tail down, and waddled toward the exit. When it butted the kickplate, the door would not budge. Cactus Pig was displeased. The tail rose up again and he turned a tight circle, squealing. Poor guy. He was as trapped as we were, and I'm afraid he blamed us for his predicament. Faron must have sensed danger for he slid to the floor and dragged me to my feet. Together we edged toward the exit as I apologized to the pig.

Outside on the savanna we hit the grass at a sprint. Even on that busted foot, Faron still outpaced me. Cactus Pig emerged behind us and bolted into the marsh. I heard a shot and turned to see a cop fire on the animal. The bullet bounced off its horny head and Cactus Pig made his escape.

Now the pistols were drawn on us. "Over here," Faron shouted. He must have been in immense pain, but he didn't let on. (He told me once that pain is only a circuit; all you needed to do was find the kill switch.)

Back in Gunt times a monorail shuttled visitors around the zoo. It soared above the enclosures in a graceful arc, giving an aerial view of nature's bounty. But the monorail was now a shipwreck. One end had collapsed and the three cars of the train had nosedived into the dirt. Faron climbed in through a busted windshield and we picked our way over the seats until we reached the level rail. This was a rounded beam thirty-odd feet off the ground. Far below I saw gazelles spray out across a meadow. They could not have been more graceful than my brother. Faron danced down the line like a housecat with a busted paw.

I fell to hands and knees. (In addition to my claustrophobia, I am also afraid of heights. The only comfortable place for me is on firm ground with plenty of open space.) I managed to hug my way forward, but Faron decided this was not a manly way to comport myself. "Up," he screamed.

We ducked under a canopy of foreign trees, bark-stripped mutants that probably pined for Madagasser or Chine. They had filthy green toes for leaves and instead of squirrels they sheltered angry little virus monkeys that shrieked at me to fall. *Fall, you little coward, fall.*

I held on until I reached the next depot. There I found Faron crouched on the platform peering through an open window. Below, a squad car idled in the bamboo.

"End of the line," said Faron.

"What?" I thought we should keep going. "Let's keep going."

"No, for real—end of the line." Faron was right. Beyond the depot the rail just stopped. He called me back to the window. Among the squad cars stood the fake man himself, the Orange Tan. He was just as they said, a potbellied child in a fringe jacket. He gazed up at us with those baleful eyes, just the hint of a smirk on his lips. End of the line, he seemed to say, for all of us.

I heard a shot and the Orange Tan sat down. The cop hadn't even bothered to get out of his car.

3.

When she returned from the clinic at midnight, was Umma surprised to find our unit vacant? Had she paused on the elevated roadway searching for my face in the eleventh-floor window? Did she wait nervously in the lobby for Faron to escort her up the stairs? Did she lie on my top bunk, as I had done so many nights, watching for two wayward boys walking up the Dixie Hiway? Did my mother already know we were not coming home?

Faron had been heading for trouble all his life, and I had followed my brother every poor turn he took just to hide behind his back. Our mother had seen this night coming for a long time.

Later she confessed how she'd return from the clinic each night half-expecting her sons would be kidnapped, dead, or shipped off to join Pop in the cane fields of Cuba. So she entered our darkened unit having anticipated everything we had done or endured. Every rude exploit and petty tragedy she had already imagined on those haunted walks home.

She lowered our bunks slowly to hear the springs expand. Her own lungs were no less pinched. Panic fed by the teaspoon, tiny gulps of air. Should she go back downstairs? Ask around the courtyard? Corner a couple of Stairdwellers and shake them down for information? Had she done so, Umma might have run across the tour guide Ross Carnation and learned from him just how fathomless the shit was that me and Faron had stepped in.

Instead she boiled water not intending to drink tea. Changing states of matter, liquid to gas—this business was almost like doing something. The stove clock passed 2:00 a.m. and we were certainly not coming home now. She stood at the kitchen bar all through the swamp-hot night, not sleeping nor moving.

Morning brought no relief. No sooner did the sun come up than a pair of thunderheads rolled in to smother the light. She opened a window and climbed my bunk to feel the rain on her face. Substitute tears. There is some wisdom in what Smart Man Tolemy said, that weather is a circulatory system of emotion, that the sky absorbs high feeling and disperses it as rain or sleet or lightning.

* * *

At that moment, me and Faron lay on another pair of bunks, provided by the Bosom Industries House of Corrections in Hiya City. For a small fee an orderly had slipped a needle in my brother's backside, and he was now sleeping off the effects of pig morphine. I kept watch on our cell's only window, high on one wall and set deep in a casement. The thunderheads that had found Umma in the Gables now pushed a black tendril into our cell. Rain spilled through the window to puddle up on the floor.

Faron looked peaceful enough. Not at all like a sociopath. The anger had flown from his open mouth and gone up into that stormy sky. In sleep my brother went gentle, and I wished that the morphine might never wear off. I came down to kneel beside him. The mat was soaked with sweat, so I rolled my brother against the block wall to cool him down. I stripped his sheet and carried it to the puddle, bringing it back heavy with rainwater to wring it over his neck and shoulders.

* * *

The door buzzer sounded. Umma jumped. She slipped from my bunk and pulled on a pair of sweatpants, stood at the peep-hole expecting it was the law. But the man who stood on our shit scraper did not look like enforcement. He was dainty, built like a resin doll, his hair so severely parted it might have been die-cut. He wore a short-sleeve shirt with a canary yellow neck-tie, his trousers more yellow still. When the stranger buzzed a second time, Umma watched how his limbs worked, as if they were hinged.

"Who are you?" she asked through the door.

He said the name Terry Nguyen and hoped this wasn't a bad time. She had been expecting a cop, but now she imagined worse. Terry Nguyen looked like an undertaker.

"I am here about your sons."

"Are they dead or in jail?"

Nguyen assured her we were alive and incarcerated.

"You are not a cop."

"I have come to help your family. Let me in."

As evidence of his sincerity, he held up a brown accordion folder. The Bosom Industries logo had been stamped across the cardstock. She opened the door. Nguyen looked so inert that he almost put our mother at ease. He was a precious object, cute but in the manner of a poison frog.

He had taken the stairs and was a bit winded, he said, though it seemed like a lie. A man in those pants would never make it past the Stairdwellers.

"Might I sit?"

She offered Faron's bottom bunk. Nguyen made no impression on the mattress. He worked one hand inside a pants pocket, twisted it as a groan issued from his throat. Umma watched the knuckles contort the fabric and heard in her mind the word *spider*. On the other hand he wore a stack of carved silver rings. Together in the tight space under my bunk, Umma said she expected the man to kiss her. He looked as if he'd been authorized to do so.

Terry began by complimenting her marks at school and record at the clinic. "High attendance. Brisk. Presentable. Improved hygiene." She'd earned good grades in Stitching as well. There was no point asking how he knew so much about her past. People know things. Nguyen wondered aloud what she hoped to accomplish when her degree was in hand.

"Stay put," she replied, not finishing the thought. She would stay put, right here in the Gables, until Pop was released from the Pens and we were a whole family again.

"Long wait that." Terry Nguyen knew about Pop.

"Yes," she said. "That is true."

"Or," he offered, "it could be quite brief."

The sentence for slaying I Murder was fourteen years plus wage garnishment for another ten. We'd be in the tower blocks forever. If Pop did live long enough to win release, he'd surely toss a Stairdweller into the airshaft and get sent down again in no time.

"How would you respond if I said your entire family could reunite, under this roof, tomorrow morning?"

Umma tried to imagine what price a man might extract for so lavish a gift. She tried to imagine what sort of man had the authority to grant it. She watched the hand twist inside its pocket and did not reply.

"You have heard of the new cruise-ship terminal up past Melburn?" he asked.

She had a hopeful thought. Maybe Nguyen would offer them indenture on an ocean liner in exchange for jail time. Bosom owned the cruise-ship terminal and the rum distillery. Prison labor could be reallocated.

"I thought they shut that terminal down?"

"They did," said Terry. He shook his little head. "Do you happen to know why?"

Umma had no clue. Melburn, Floriday, was a good bit north of Miamy.

"I asked them to." Terry said this proudly, though his expression did not change. He explained: a crew had been hammering through cement slab when their front loader dropped into a sinkhole. Not an unusual occurrence. Floriday was always opening up. They lowered a man down to retrieve the vehicle and he found a tunnel. Next he found a chamber, and then an ancient storehouse the size of a salt mine.

"Someone had sealed it off with cement, covered their tracks with sand so no one would find it, as if they had something to protect." He held his breath. Umma felt compelled to join him. "There's a . . . vehicle down there."

He spoke this last bit in a hush, a furry tone of reverence. He must have been disappointed when Umma glared at his tiny feet in annoyance. If our mother ever felt reverence, she concealed it, capped her feelings with cement slab, and hid them under a pile of sand. She only wanted to know what any of this had to do with getting her sons back.

It did not ease her irritation when Terry turned the conversation to fairy tales. "You have heard of the Astronomers?" he asked, though of course she had. Everyone had.

You, Little Sylvia, will come up knowing the truth, but to the rest of the world—to jellyfishers, crackers, finkies, and swells, to Bosom families and Consolidated alike—the stars are not real. The planets are not real. Astronomy, if spoken of at all, is regarded as a delusional cult scarcely more respectable than the Jesus Lovers. The Chiefs long back did the decent thing and decided to put both gangs out of business. The Jesus Lovers dug in; you still see their lowercase *t* scratched on fenceposts with a ten-dollar nail. But the Astronomers went off quietly and without leaving a trace or sign.

They were easily dispatched because their ideas so nearly resembled fiction. You will learn better, Little Sylvia, but to the rest of the world Astronomy is nonsense, magic on par with weather-knowing and poetry cures.

The surest way to hobble any truth is to put it in a story-book. Smart Man Tolemy wrote *The Lonesome Wanderer* for children so that we would come up knowing Astronomy as a fairy tale. His Astronomers were pale, hairless mountain men who believed the bright flaws in the Night Glass to be distant Suns. They believed the Wanderers to be other worlds like our own. In contradiction of common sense and observation, their Sun did not circle the Earth but the other way around.

In *The Lonesome Wanderer* every planet was equal; we were one of many, insignificant. Tolemy's Astronomers worshipped the Wanderers as flying mansions for the gods. Every child was urged to learn their names:

Mercury, the Messenger's swift chariot built of glowing embers.

Earth, prison of Man, a god of guilt who gnaws at the walls of his cell.

Mars, with canals like Sunk Venice, where Strife pilots her warship.

Venus, a brothel for the gods, kept by the Virgin Madam.

Saturn, girded by a belt of seeds for sowing the crops of Earth.

Jupiter, a hot-air balloon piloted by the Great Chief Jesus. Neptune and Uranus, the poison-misted plains of the Ice Giants.

There had been an Eighth Wanderer as well: far Pluto, House of Death—so despised by the Astronomers that they forbid its name to be spoken aloud. This was Tolemy's Lonesome Wanderer, and to its forgotten surface he consigned the fool Astronomers.

Though I cannot say for certain, I believe it was the Smart Man himself who dismantled all the telescopes. He did so to prevent the world from knowing the truth: that the Astronomers were not fools, they were right.

"Only there is more to that story than what Smart Man Tolemy wrote down," said Terry. "Were you aware that Floriday herself was a site held sacred to Astronomy? Right north of Melburn is a cape of land called Cannibal where they practiced sacrifice to the Wanderers, fire rites. When that hole opened up in the cement slab, our front loader fell crack into the antechamber of their holiest temple."

"That right?"

"In their final days the Gunts believed their world was coming to an end, and soon. They went to the mountain to ask the Astronomers what could be done."

The wise men gazed into their glasses and saw a vision: by the Wanderer Jupiter lay a moon that was one shoreless ocean frozen over like the shell of an egg. They named it after a failed Gunt social experiment where the maps now show Bosomland.

Europa. Wet and teeming with life under the ice, it would be a new Earth when this one had been spent. Go back down the mountain, the Astronomers instructed. Build an airplane tall as the Four Seasons Miamy. Call it Orion after a famous outdoorsman. Bury it, they told the Gunts, deep in the sands of Floriday, and wait.

"Wait for what?"

"When the end date of the world is fixed and forty days at hand, said the Astronomers, the Chiefs will pass from the Earth."

Umma laughed. Everyone knew the Chiefs were not going anywhere.

"On that day," Terry continued, "Orion will rise up and fly away to Europa. But the Gunts were wrong: it wasn't our world that ended. It was theirs."

A withered part of Umma had always wanted the Astronomers to be real. On Caroline nights, while sleep overtook us in our sharecropper tents, she would sit up in her underpants on an old lounger to watch the stars come out. She longed to see worlds in the Wanderers, suns in the starlight. Umma came from superstitious stock, Appellatians and Jesus Lovers, and old ideas can clog the tubes like dead leaves in a drainpipe. When Terry talked his nonsense about Europa and Orion and escape, she listened as if under a spell. Then she remembered.

"You know where my boys are at?" said Umma. "You promised you would help."

Terry told her to be patient. He was getting to her boys. But first, he wanted tea. A splash was left over from yesterday's breakfast. She brought it to him in a mustard jar, which he accepted with a gesture of thanks as inert as his smile.

"I persuaded Bosom to halt construction on the cruise terminal until we knew what we were looking at down there. The vehicle is called Orion and I believe it is built to fly. The Gunts were good craftsmen. They left behind thorough instructions for how to launch it, and I intend to do so." Now he got to the sugar-pith, as Pop would say, inside the cane. "The trouble, Miss Van Zandt, has been in recruiting volunteers."

"Volunteers? Doesn't Bosom have pilots?"

Nguyen paid her a compliment. Good, strong tea. "Your family possesses so many of the qualities we seek," he said. "Doctor schooling, a hardy husband, two sons who have performed adequately on their mining exams."

"Thank you," she said.

"But mostly," said Terry, "what you have is motive. You will want to do it."

Umma understood that this was no longer a conversation. Nguyen could afford to frighten her. "I am authorized by Bosom Industries to extend the following offer," he said. "You agree to train for and test the Orion; we grant amnesty to your husband and sons."

From his accordion folder he extracted a sheaf of legal papers. The hand appeared from its pocket clicking a pen.

"Can you tell me what my boys have done?"

For the first time since Terry Nguyen entered the apartment, Umma saw the man who sat beside her. She counted the fingers on the hand that held the pen: three. A salmon-colored scar ran from his wrist to the base of his middle finger. The skin above one ear was discolored, yellow. He wore a hairpiece, half a wig.

"Your husband has already given his assent." With his pinkie he tapped a line at the bottom of the first page, then slipped it back in the folder before she could get a good look. "So have your sons."

So it was that Umma signed her name and made her choice: between probable death and guaranteed loneliness. She could not have chosen otherwise, because, daughter, there is only one ending worse than the grave.

* * *

I shook my brother awake. Another night had passed, and the turnkey had come to set us free. She didn't mention the terms of our release. Discussion was limited to ordinals: left, right, forward, up, out. As Hiya City daylight appeared through the door, my brother underwent a miraculous recovery. His steps grew spritelier, the angry egg on his forehead less gooselike. He swaggered.

I slowed down, worried. Whatever we were being released to could not be freedom. Had we not but forty-eight hours earlier driven a stolen bus into a gator nest? Had we not inconvenienced or possibly killed a number of geriatrics in our flight from the law? The turnkey shoved us onto a scrubbed Hiya sidewalk and bolted the prison door behind us.

We were welcomed back into the world by a most unfriendly mob of grannies. They clustered on the opposite curb, shouting crude footnotes to the placards they held over their heads.

I AM NOT GATOR FOOD!

DEATH TO THE MIAMY ZOO TWO!

One lady threatened to gut me like a fish and then specified what fish and how she would cook my fillets.

We might run, but this was Hiya City, and geriatrics were everywhere. When the wind shifted I could smell their dusty perfume. They started shuffling across the street on their evil aluminum walkers. The elderly are a danger because they are past consequence and have permission to behave like dogs. I shrank behind Faron.

Before the angry mob overcame us, a black golf cart puttered up to the curb. In its smoked-glass windows I saw our own sorry reflections. The passenger door swung open, and a man leaned out as far as his seat belt would allow. "Give you a lift?"

The driver was Terry Nguyen. From a cooler under the seat he offered us drink boxes in purple and orange. I took orange; Faron declined. At the Hiya gatehouse Terry waved at a guard. The striped arm lifted and we were let go from that exurb of death.

So why was my hand still shaking so hard? I could scarcely poke the sharpened straw through the membrane of my juice box.

We puttered out onto the Dixie Hiway, leaving behind the order and hygiene of Hiya City. The elevated roadway was buckled and broken. Exit ramps ended in marsh—marsh that extended for miles on either side, filling the air with the rank odors of vegetal sex and rot. There is no civilizing low tide, I suppose.

Nguyen explained to us the terms Umma and Pop had agreed to, what it would mean for our family should we decline. No release for Pop; the Gables for Umma; life in Cuba for me and Faron.

It was the most preposterous thing I'd ever heard: blast a hole in the Night Glass to visit a make-believe moon. I was sure it would fail, but I should have been worried about success as well. What if we actually made the trip and had to live on a great big snowball? But if Umma had signed and Pop, too, there must have been something in it. I said yes.

Faron wanted to have a look at the paperwork. Nguyen handed over a pile of waivers and contracts. My brother pretended to read them, then he unlatched the window and let the papers flap out over the marsh like filthy white birds.

If Nguyen took offense, he did not show it. All he did was to ease onto the shoulder and stop. He threw open the passenger door.

"I have what I require from your family," he said. "If you do not wish to accompany them, you are free to find your own way."

I looked out over the soggy plain of sawgrass, the cypress groves in shipwrecked malls. Looked ahead to where the hiway ended at the Miamy Ruins. I said that I wouldn't go anywhere without my brother; neither would Pop or Umma, no matter what they had signed.

Nguyen showed me a labored smile. It seemed to linger in the rearview mirror, even as he turned to address us.

"I was the only one who thought your brother suitable for this undertaking," he said. "I spoke up on his behalf. Now I see that I should not have bothered."

The heat was rising. It gave the insects something to chat about. A fan whirred under the hood. The sense was of a mechanical conspiracy, of cogs that click and compound eyes that parcel up the world: what was needed, what was not. Faron was fixing to be spat out.

"Go on. Get out. You may try to run," said Nguyen. "But I suggest you save your strength and wait here for them to pick you up." He took a walky-talk from the glove box and spoke in a deferential tone. He seemed to be asking permission; a choice must be made and Terry did not have the clearance to make it. Faron snatched the walky-talk from Nguyen's crippled hand.

"I will kill you," my brother screamed into the radio. "After you, I will kill your Chief. Next I kill his Chief and his, and then all the way up the pole till it's just me on top and you are all as gone as Gunts!"

I felt at that moment that we had passed a threshold. A choice had been made. This was not a sport and there were no ties. There would be no point in persuading Faron to sign those papers now, I thought. Nguyen was not the sort to allow second chances. It was the Cuba Pens for us, the Gables for Umma. Pop was a dead man.

Then Faron's voice went quiet. His snarl flattened. He blinked. He said, "Yes, sir." Tears came as he handed me the radio.

I started into my usual speech: my brother was good; he was. "He likes to shout is all." But if I could just talk Faron down, I was sure he would sign those papers and no further trouble might be expected from us.

"Rowan."

It was Pop on the other end.

"Where are you?" I said.

"In the Gables. You have made the right decision," he said. I heard friction, the red roughness of Pop's beard. I pictured him rubbing it, trying to adjust his big crazy head to the new circumstance. "Sign the papers and come on home," he said. "Your ma will be relieved to see you."

4.

WE GATHERED THAT NIGHT IN THE GABLES FOR A BIG feed. It was a reunion and a bon voyage both. Umma made roast goose, fatty-meat sausage, yams, and her own papaya salad spiked with wasp chillies. She had borrowed four stools from a neighbor. The card table was covered with a striped yellow cloth I didn't know we owned. She said sit down quick because one leg was buckling under the weight of all the dishes. Pop supported the corner with his knee and chopped off a segment of sausage. The fat drained out on the trip to his plate, but he dabbed it up with a slice of bread. Umma joined us with two jugs of Haven Dark, and the family ate and drank till we got gassy, belchy, and bully wasted.

While she washed dishes Pop fired up a weed. He touched the one-hitter pipe to my mother's lips. Her hands sank in greasy water but her eyes wandered free. She wanted to go anywhere but here, this last night. Pop and Faron were braced for anything; I was afraid; Umma, she was only sad. We folded

up the card table and lowered my brother's bunk to make a
sofa. We had one closet in that apartment, a vestibule really,
hung with an Oriental bathrobe. Pop rummaged inside and
by the humming under his breath we knew what he was looking for. We had not had a family sing-along for a year, and
though I was no performer, I missed the together feeling when
Pop busted out his Roland AX.

After a few minutes he had his rig all set up. Pop was rusty,
but he played so loud and grinned so broad you couldn't complain. From a hand-copied songbook he picked out tunes from
the days of our ancestors. His people had come from West
Texas, and they were musical cowboys with drug problems.
One great-great something-or-other had written a number of
sad and strange ballads, a few comedy songs in the "talking
blues" style that was tremendously popular at the time. I have
heard the man himself only once, in a degraded recording, and
he could not sing. Still, there was a miserable strain to his voice
that made you feel you were the only one left in the world who
was listening. I do not know how this ancestral Van Zandt
looked, but I picture the Fake Man, an Orange Tan with a guitar singing about all the things that are easier than waiting
around to die.

Pop was proud of his Roland AX. He loved to sing its
praises. Generations of musicians had worn grooves in its pitch-
bend wheel; the case was crazed with age and exposure. He
had restored it using vintage parts and improvised electron-
ics. The neck, which he'd fractured in two places, he had
mended with plastic sealant. He polished its sparkle black

finish after every sing-along. Part of the fun was watching him work its keys with a roll of toilet paper and a bottle of Old English, knowing those injurious hands of his could care for something, too.

My father was born in Houston but did not remain there long. The Van Zandts had always been a Bosom Industries family, and they lived in a Bosom condo block. His pa, Oak, worked as a fisherman in the Mexy Gulf. In those days the water boiled with flavorful sea life, like soup. Saltbats, sargasso snakeheads, and delicate tubeworms you could eat like licorice whips. Oak worked mostly on jellyboats, and Pop said he hauled in tons of that sweet translucent flesh to sell in the Yucatan Company commissaries. The deal was to sign on for three-week runs and come home months later with thousand-dollar bills stuffed in your boots.

Not even Grandma knew when he was coming home. He'd burst through their front door and fall to his knees, throw his arms wide for a hug, but Pop would always hide behind the loveseat. He was afraid of his daddy's arms, so red from the stings, so puffed up that they resembled a pair of fatty-meat sausages. Oak would laugh at his boy's cowardice, chase him around the den till he caught him, and then Pop would fall asleep on his father's belly, smelling wrack and money. Whenever Umma served fatty-meats we were treated to another story about Grandpa Oak. Never heard much about Grandma.

The story Pop told that last night in the Gables was terrible sad with a hopeful ending. It was the summer before my father turned ten. Oak needed the cash so he took a late-season job with a rival outfit, Consolidated Fisheries. A string of shark rigs ran the length of a sunken island called Gallstone. The trap was brutal and clever: four metal rods protruded from a cement piling, bait balls attached to the end of each one. Those rods carried 20,000 volts of electricity delivered from a generator on the platform. Oak and his partner worked them like crab pots, boating from one platform to the next to goose the generators, load the rods, and collect fried sharks from the sandy bottom.

Whatever rig they had reached by nightfall, that is where they would camp out. Every time a shark got zapped, an orange signal lamp flared. Grandpa said it was near impossible to sleep.

He had taken a long weekend home in Houston before setting out for his second rotation of the season. First night back on the job, the dispatcher urged them to hurry through their rounds. A tropical was bearing down on the Texas coast and the Chief wanted to gather as much shark meat as he could in case his rigs blew down.

By the time they reached the last platform, the swells were so high, they couldn't see the pilings. They tied off as best they could and radioed the dispatcher. The job was done but they would have to hunker down on the platform for the night. The dispatcher suggested they tether themselves to the ironwork tower. Oak told the man he intended to cut the boat loose; if it blew onto the platform, they might be crushed. The dispatcher refused to authorize; doing so would be a breach of contract. Consolidated Fisheries would no longer be responsible for their welfare.

"Nobody will come for you," he said.

The following morning a Consolidated grief counselor arrived to notify the family in Houston. Called himself "Gene from settlement." He stepped in funeral brogans over broken glass and chewed-up branches. The storm had made a mess of the condo complex. A Fanta machine lay at the bottom of the pool; a slow leak turning the water a pale orange. He employed a respectful knocking rhythm learned from the Consolidated book of comportment: knock, pause, knock-knock. Grandma answered the door, then excused herself, leaving Gene to wait on the shit scraper. She did not return.

Pop was the only boy among five older sisters. After their pa died his mother elected not to look at him anymore. People had always compared Pop to Oak; it was a compliment. But now the resemblance left him motherless. He started hitting the road and having adventures. Every time he got lonely, bored, or broke he would slink back to Houston where his ma would pretend he had not entered the room. Finally, at age fourteen, Pop set off on his last long run.

He learned to pick soybeans and poppy and peaches and to live in a tent or a bunkhouse or sleep on a barge. Migrant farming brought him east. Once you got in the tubes of Bosom Ag, the company would take you on wherever it was harvest time, even if you came from Texas. Gradually he picked his way around the Mexy Gulf and down into Floriday, where his happiest weeks were spent. Pop was a rowdy teen living rough in the orange groves. He fished cat in the rivers and ate what he wanted from the branches. At the end of the harvest he rode north with some boys to look for work in a So Caroline textile mill. When he saw the painted-over windows of that block building, he thought, with the finality of the young, that the good times were finished. A certain type of man spends his youth sure it will end by the week after next. But the truth was, happiness had just begun for Pop. It was in that textile mill that he met Umma.

Her people had been Consolidated War & Jail partisans for generations, so loyal that they had ascended to middle management. Umma's father was a man named Coylan Howard and he oversaw the cutting room. When Pop turned up seeking employment, Coylan could tell right off he was a Bosom man, so he offered him the dreariest job on the floor. All day long he'd spool fabric off an unwinding truck and layer it across a table. When a buzzer sounded Coylan would guide a saw along a chalk path, hacking out twenty pieces at a time. Pop had to load the cuts on a cart and wheel them into a long hall where ladies clicked away on sewing machines. He said the racket in that room sounded like seven-year locusts telling gossip. After the sewing was done, Pop boxed the jumpsuits and a truck took them to Miamy to meet a boat bound for the Cuba Pens. In this fashion, Consolidated dressed a hundred new prisoners a week. Some weeks they did soldiers; same jumpsuits, he said, different patches.

Umma worked in the sewing hall but the ladies all knew it was temporary. If she didn't screw up, she was guaranteed to make manager like her father. With Pop's help, Umma screwed up fast. When she started to show, he took her on the road. A weed plantation in No Caroline was hiring bud pickers.

* * *

That last night in the Gables, Umma called the tune: one of those sweet miserable ballads from Pop's ancestor, a song about staying put and never going anywhere in search of anything because there was nothing out there to find. Pop planted a foot on the amp, slung the strap over his head, and rested his right palm on the keyboard. He leaned into the hook so that it sounded like a flute made of soft rubber. He kneaded the notes, stretched them till you thought they might snap. Umma sang quiet and true, how she didn't need nothing. She sang directly at me, telling me I better pray that they never find me. My back, she said, was not strong enough. Umma sang to me about the precious things. Sorrow and solitude: the only words that are worth remembering.

5.

NEXT MORNING ALL WE WANTED WAS TO SLEEP THE
rum and goose fat out of our tubes. All I wanted was to rise
at my own leisure to Pop's drowsy laughter and dig into a pan
of scramble with dry toast. But the fist on the door was persistent. Not loud, only regular. I wedged my head under the
pillow and woke up minutes later gasping for air.

Outside I heard the super's voice. This man was eelish, wore
a slender eel of a mustache, and spoke in a wet hiss. I heard
him apologize to someone in the hall; most families in the
Gables were decent, but others, well . . . the door swung open,
and the super swept one arm across our living space to show
Terry Nguyen how far some tenants could fall below the
threshold of decency. "Welcome to the Four Seasons, Captain."

While Nguyen took the liberty of boiling tea water, Umma
rolled off the air mattress with a deflated sound. She crawled
on all fours to Pop's amp and rested her head there a while
before crossing the room to lean against the breakfast bar.

"The van," Nguyen told her, "is waiting downstairs. And has been for close to an hour." Perhaps, he suggested without malice, we had forgotten to set our alarm.

Because no one else stirred, I felt it incumbent on me to come to Umma's aid. This took some doing. When I sat up the hangover expanded in my skull like a pine cone. Having arranged the kettle, our unwelcome guest strolled about the unit, inspecting every inch. Houseflies browsed inside the goose carcass. Pop snored on, the Roland slung around his heaving chest. Nguyen fingered the one-hitter, carried our empty jugs to the sink, and made a demonstration out of tidying up.

I studied his face for a judgment. Would he frown? Wince? Chastise us? Rescind his most generous offer to blast us bodily at the solid sky? Nguyen's face remained as impassive as ever, a picture of itself. My brother was offered the first cup of tea, a gesture, I suppose, meant to smooth over the previous day's friction. Legs sprawled, one bent knee pressed against the wall, Faron pretended to sleep. But his teeth were set and the lashes twitched. "Drink up," said Nguyen, setting the warm mug on Faron's leg. My brother opened one eye. "We have a long ride ahead of us."

I looked for the golf cart in the parking lot, but Terry had engaged a far more splashy ride for this momentous day. His white Darling Vanster featured three rows of seats, front and rear bumpers, and a handsome pebbled-vinyl dash. On the road to Cape Cannibal we made little in the way of conversation. We each contemplated our separate miseries and aired our individual gases. Nguyen rolled down every window but his own. His delicate movements, I realized, were on account of that hairpiece. For a man who reveals nothing, the loss of a wig must be intolerable.

The freeway tumbled by under intense sun, past Hiya City, where I slunk low in my seat. Up the coast the world grew more peopled and its commerce less practical. We passed discount flooring shops and private nightclubs with names like the Duck Inn and the Boiler Room, a shooting range called Head Woundz. A guy dressed as scissors waved at us from the parking lot of a haircuttery. Pop waved back. I tried to imagine the lavish lives of midstate Floridayans, their busy social calendars, the firearms and paid-for hairstyles, the colorful tiled floors.

Nguyen turned off where the sign read CRUISE SHIP TERMINAL. Indian River, deep carved and sheltered from the sea, is a traditional port of call for these magnificent vessels. I remember a white liner standing tall over the cranes, sleek and poetic. Pop wondered aloud at the cost of such a ship, at the wealth of its passengers. Nguyen made no comment, only pushed on past the terminals to the interior of the cape.

Here the blacktop fell to pieces. Bubbled, sank, pimpled up, and boiled forth sand. Palmettos had pushed through the asphalt, requiring some deft steering, which Nguyen handled with minimal fuss. We came upon a crowd of turkey vultures picking at a flat whitetail. He blew the horn and they fluttered into the air, in no special hurry, only to settle back down to lunch after we'd passed. The road turned to concrete slab, an improvement and indication that the route had once borne heavy payloads. On the right appeared a clutch of rotted buildings. The sign read VISITORS CENTER. Dented missiles lay around in a pile like cigarette butts. Grackles stood on the nose cones, lords of all that busted potential.

From a distance the security gate looked bully enough, but when we drew close I saw that it was nothing more than a plywood cabana borrowed from a private beach. The guard rested her squirrel popper on a sawhorse. At the sight of Terry Nguyen she dragged the barricade onto the shoulder, taking her time. Under her reflective vest I saw that she wore a spine brace.

"That your muscle?" Pop asked Terry. He was getting his spark back, which concerned me.

Nguyen told him this headland used to be a walled city, a fortress. The Astronomers named it after a Gunt warrior priest called Jack Kennedy. This man had declared war on all Commies. They'd had a spat about who adored the Moon more, Terry explained, so Jack and the Reds settled it with a gentleman's wager: whoever reached it first would be most beloved by heaven. To protect his facility from the Commies, Kennedy's Space Center was gated off, like Hiya City. Had its own power supply, water, and police. They hid all the secret stuff inside a gator-infested swamp.

Terry pointed out three good-sized bulls in the culvert. "Now," he said, "the whole place belongs to those monsters." When they were clearing land for the cruise-ship terminal, every foreman was required to carry a shotgun, "and we still lost three men."

The world goes wild so fast, I thought. The flattop dipped in and out of black water, and the Vanster struggled. Pine trunks stood blanched and headless in the wake of a hurrycane. The only sign of habitation was a single edifice that rose among the scrub palms like an ocean liner run aground. A factory and warehouse, Nguyen explained, the grandest in the Gunt world, for storing their holy missiles.

At a small gravel road he turned off into the woods. We crossed the culvert on a makeshift bridge of tractor tires and scrap lumber. In a clearing the white warehouse loomed overhead. You could still make out a faded Gunt flag and the cultish blue emblem of the Astronomers writ huge on its facade. But when Terry edged around back, we saw how low this cathedral had sunk.

The rear of the building had been shredded by storms and melted by fire. You could see inside from the floor clear up to the ruined roof. Nguyen told us it was the largest one-story building ever made. Neat mounds of rubble had been bull-dozed out to the perimeter, but the rubbish crew was now gone and their earth movers rusted under blue tarps.

Attached to the warehouse was a four-story structure that appeared largely intact. "Launch Control." Nguyen idled in front of the lobby. "This is where the Astronomers made their sacrifices to the Moon, where they sent tributes to the Wan-derers," only to watch their bright missiles crash against the Night Glass.

He spun the van about and carried on past a stand of bleachers and low black buildings. These were for "the lower

Astronomers, Gunt functionaries, come to admire the sacrifices." The road we were on paralleled a second, broader thoroughfare that was paved down two sides with unbroken bands of concrete. The median had been filled in with crushed bluestone. Pop asked if it was a runway.

"We think it was a road," said Nguyen. "For a colossal truck they called the Crawler. It was how they carried the missiles from the warehouse to the launchpad."

Umma grew more agitated the farther we traveled. Her hands wanted a job to do. They dug into the upholstery like she was prospecting for loose change.

The Crawler Road veered off to our left. I saw where it ended at a flattop mound penetrated by a great concrete trough. Faron pointed to a structure on top, an openwork scaffold or antenna.

"Launchpad 39B," said Nguyen. "Take a good look. This is the last acre of Earth your feet are going to stand on."

Umma spoke for the first time, her voice small enough to get Terry's attention.

"Are we a sacrifice?" she said.

He pushed on through a bog of scrub palms and onto a dirt road. "Miss Van Zandt," Terry said. "Bear in mind that everything I tell you is a fairy tale. Or perhaps it isn't."

"Did they ever make it through, though?" By which she meant through the Night Glass.

Nguyen braked in a clearing between two elegant motor homes. "Here we are!" He honked to disperse the turkey vultures and got out to show us around our new lodgings.

Someone had dressed up the door with a wreath of Spanish moss. Our surname was stenciled in red on the polyvinyl. Nguyen turned a key and tried the knob with his diminished hand but it wouldn't budge. By the van Umma made a circle like a mutt trying to settle in, then sat in the grass. Pop strode up and checked the door with his shoulder. I heard the old weather stripping rip free.

"My wife is not feeling well," he said.

I shut my eyes and smelled my way inside the motor home. The interior reeked of wet canvas, a smell I particularly loved, for it reminded me of tent living in the peach orchards. Terry Nguyen found the light switch, and Pop whistled appreciatively, for Umma's benefit. She followed us in.

"See here, doll. I told you Bosom would put us up in style."

He was right. This was utter luxury. The dine-in kitchen had about fifteen styles of veneer, each one a studied facsimile of some natural surface. The double sink looked new. It was offset by a marbled backsplash with hooks for scrub brushes and oven mitts. There was no oven—who would bake bread in this heat?—but the full range had a built-in timer and a center eye exclusively for pancakes.

Pop slipped out of his boots and moaned. The carpet was resolutely shag, in the corporate colors of Bosom Industries, yellow and brighter yellow. Through a beaded curtain Terry revealed the master bedroom. I had never seen a Californdulia king outside a catalog and could not resist giving it the old bounce test. "Come on, Faron," I said. He joined in, but only to give Umma a laugh. On either side of the bed, matching lamps stood on built-in nightstands. They had been artfully formed in resin to represent some species of mythical sea beast.

"Manatees," Nguyen said. "The original Floridayans killed them for sport, with motorboats."

A shelf atop the headboard groaned with paper books. Terry Nguyen told me they had been found in a bunker beneath Launch Control. These volumes, he said, represented the private library of an ancient Astronomer called Bob Sprell. "He must have been a vastly wealthy man."

From the stacks he offered me a paperback. "You look like a reader." His selection had not been arbitrary. *The First Men in the Moon* was its title, and Mr. H. G. Wells the man who wrote it. The story took the fanaticism of the Astronomers into the realm of madness. There used to be Jesus Lovers in the Gables. They would enter their trances right there in the lobby and embarrass everyone. They shouted and sang to the Fanta machine in a homemade language, did so with narrowed eyes and lolling gray tongues—with such crisp articulation that you almost believed they saw something you didn't. H. G. Wells must have been one of them, and his book a seizure of belief.

"Hey, look at that! You like a good reading book, too, hon," Pop said.

I could take no more of his attempts to coax Umma out of her gloom, so I climbed into the padded loft above the master bedroom with Mr. Wells and his moon bugs. Better company. A skylight showed the cool blue of late morning. A gull shot past, giving the loft the sensation of flight. Below I heard

Nguyen say good-bye. Faron joined me in the loft, and pretty soon the snoring was general across our pretty new home.

Noon came and the great Peeping Tom of the sun crawled into view. While the rest of my family slept, I lost myself in the old plastic dome of the skylight, in its network of tiny fractures brightened by the sun. As a boy, I looked everywhere for patterns. Patterns held the world together or did the opposite.

Our siesta was interrupted too soon by Terry Nguyen's three-finger knock. Lunchtime. Under a sickly black oak he showed us a picnic table laid with cold cuts, cheese singles, sacks of snowy white bread, a tub of macaroni salad, and iced tea in pitchers. Beers floated in a styrofoam cooler. If we were human sacrifices, Terry intended to fatten us up like calves.

We weren't the only livestock invited to lunch. Butt to butt on the opposite bench sat a family that looked almost as shitted-out as the Van Zandts.

Terry started the introductions with Mae Reade. She was my own mother's age, but where Umma's hardness radiated heat, Mae appeared to be frozen solid. She smiled with greater conviction on one side of her face than the other. Her chin showed a bruise, but so did her knuckles. She lavished mayo on a disk of boiled ham, not rising to shake Pop's extended hand.

Bill Reade was her husband. He wore sunglasses and a straw hat and sat upright like the decorated soldier he had once been. There was no kindly feature on his face. He seemed like a man who delivered bad news for a living, went door-to-door with no other intention than to crush your dreams. I disliked him on sight.

The girl who sat between them, on the other hand, was someone I could look at forever. Not that she was overly pretty. One of her ears was tattooed green, which is how I learned that the Reades hailed from Canaday. Her hair had been buzzed close to her scalp some days before and had grown back in oddly spaced whorls like there was no consensus about the way forward. I wanted to gather those knots between my fingers and comb that mangled head with my hand.

I do not know what the girl thought about me. She folded a slice of bread and bit a hole in the middle. Then she unfolded it and glared at us through the hole. Faron stared back at her, and I felt for the first time the pinch of fraternal envy. I know it might be hard to believe, but I rarely envied my brother. I was content to take cover behind him for the rest of my life.

"What's her name?" he asked.

"Who?" said Nguyen. He was dishing out macaroni salad.

"That one there."

"How insensitive of me," said Terry. "Meet the Reades' daughter, Sylvia."

At Pop's urging I tried to make conversation. I cannot recall the first thing I ever said to Sylvia Reade. I only know that it took me a long time to say it. When I was finished she looked at me and said, "Are you going to talk like that the whole time?"

She winged the slice of bread into the bushes and stalked back inside her trailer. To my father Bill Reade said something unkind about the temperament of daughters. He winked at me. Umma stared into the cooler.

It was just as well Sylvia had left the picnic. I was feeling the initial stages of the shits. Even as I sat down to those rich boiled meats, my tubes went knotty. I mean no offense to the food. We had not seen such a spread in our whole lives. My discomfort was on account of the contrast. Everything last night's simple family dinner had been, this fancy outdoor luncheon was not: no laughter, no song, no solidarity. Only the flap of the palm fronds and the sound of compulsory chewing. I excused myself to pass the rest of the afternoon in our private toilet.

6.

WHEN LUNCH HAD RUN ITS COURSE I VENTURED OUT-
side again, pulling the door tight against the odor of my anx-
iety. Terry Nguyen sat behind the wheel of his Darling Vanster.
He clucked the horn and waved us over. We were to enjoy a
grand tour of Kennedy's Space Center, starting at Launch
Control.

He parked beside a mound of soggy drywall and we
entered through a plastic tarp that hung over the doors. The
lobby, littered with bits of glass, Terry called an antechamber. He did love that word. A faded mural covered one wall:
ghostly winged craft and gleaming sharp missiles floated
around colored globes. A thickset human form with a fish-
bowl for a head towered over the quarter Moon. Bill Reade
studied this man intently, wagging a finger as if he recognized him.

I was drawn to the wall opposite, where triangles of clean
white showed in the dingy stucco. Plaques had once hung

there, said Terry, but he declined to tell what they'd commemorated. I know now: each one recalled a space flight—carrying humans, virus monkeys, or machines—to the Moon, past Mercury, or into the rings of Saturn. Some craft are out there still, scaling the mountains of Mars or sprinting through interstellar space.

Down a cinder-block hallway, we were shown the auditorium where we would receive our morning lectures and evening recaps. It had probably been a snack room, but Nguyen had dressed it up with a projector and dry-erase board like a proper classroom. Pop, who had never seen the inside of a schoolhouse, bounced on his toes and said well, well. The folding seats had apparently been pried out of a multiplex. Our names, and others, had been stenciled on the backs, assigned seating. Nguyen invited Pop to experience the spring action, and he was glad to oblige. The bolts strained against the floor as he settled in for a good sit. He declared the upholstery to be soft beyond words. This was how the old man behaved when he was kind. He overpraised, abused his intensifiers. He talked with his hands like a borderline dandy so that you sometimes wished he'd go back to breaking legs.

One flight up we toured the makeshift gymnasium. Terry fiddled with a boom box until the music of old Miamy filled the air. In its prime, Cape Cannibal must have been alive with music. How the Doctors of Astronomy would have danced to the rhythms of jet propulsion and stepped to the red pulse of countdown clocks. I saw their spirits sway among the treadmills and Pilates balls.

The cardio room contained its usual implements of false hope, a bike with no wheels, sandbags to be toted from here to there and back again, a rowboat that went nowhere. (Sylvia drew a circle on the wall in front of the rowing machine and wrote "yourope" underneath. You could pull till you shat your uniform but that Moon never got any closer.) There was one device I could not identify. It looked like the sort of kinetic sculpture you find in an outlet mall food court. Terry called it his Gyro, like the sandwich. Three rings as wide as Pop's outstretched arms were hitched together with gimbals to allow free motion in all directions. Nested inside them was a padded black throne with straps and grips.

"Custom-built," said Nguyen, "from a three-hundred-year-old blueprint."

I have before me on my desk at Paranal a textbook plate depicting a similar device, though much older and more artful. Léon Foucault designed his gyroscope to measure the Earth's rotation. Terry's contraption gauged the limits of human nausea.

He asked if anyone wanted to take a spin. Bill Reade looked at the rest of us and sucked his teeth. I wasn't about to sit inside that thing until I'd been forced to. Bill, however, was emerging as our alpha, our rock, a role Pop seemed content to let him fill. Faron snorted out a laugh when Bill stooped inside the Gyro. He was cinched into the shoulder harness and it was suggested that he keep his hands on the grips. "There is a minimal risk of limb loss," said Terry.

When the hoops were given a spin, Bill's body whirled in three directions at once while his expression held fast, a smirk tight enough to contain the vomit that had no doubt accumulated behind his lips. He turned green and then white but did not demand to get off. Here is all you need to know about Bill Reade: that man was only satisfied when the world was spinning around him. And in his eyes, at that moment, we were only satellites of Bill.

On the third floor we received a tour of Launch Control proper. The old key-card box had been hammered flat. Terry opened a padlock and a heavy chain slid to the floor. Inside the room called to mind a burnt-out House of Jesus me and Faron ran across in a weed field. Launch Control had pews, an altar, and a rose window of sorts to gaze out upon the immortal. The lower clergy would have sat behind the banks of telephones and computer screens. Blue placards identified each Astronomer by rank and purpose: PAYLOAD MANAGER; PURGE, VENT, AND DRAIN; HAZ GAS.

Their consoles faced a carpeted dais upon which sat the High Astronomers. On either side were glass enclosures that Terry called the Bubbles, and they were reserved for only the guntiest of Gunts.

But the holiest of holy? That happened out there, beyond the impact-resistant windows. Down the Crawler Road you could see clear to the Launchpad. LED clocks set in every wall ticked off the inevitable red seconds till liftoff: WINDOW REMAINING, COUNTDOWN, POST LOX DRAINBACK

ELAPSED TIME. With the push of a button, Terry started our clock right then and there: 304:00:00:00. The Julian calendar: no months, just an endless scroll of days.

Back in the van I was seated beside Bill, so close that the hairs on his arm tickled mine. I felt them work inside me, the cilia of a caterpillar. I thought then that it was his bravery trying to penetrate my skin. He wanted to infect me with his manly substance, overpower me with it, and thereby harden my resolve for what lay ahead. I shrank against the door. I wanted to be brave like I wanted to be dead.

Bill stared ahead into Terry's rearview mirror and by process of reflection into my eyes. Under the brim of his stupid straw hat, his own eyes were at once too big and too small. Whites as fat as boiled eggs, corneas shrunken and the palest blue. He appeared to be blind and astonished at the same time.

Bill asked me what I was "into." It was the sort of aimless question you ask a boy you don't care to converse with. I replied that I did not know, but Bill was no longer listening. Pop answered for me in a loud voice. "History," he said, so proud. "Most boys play hooky to smoke a weed or squeeze on the girlies. Not my boy. Rowan here gives guided bus tours of historical landmarks out of the kindness of his heart."

Bill pretended alarm at hearing this. "I have always considered," his assault began, "that our past is but an inferior version of the present. A rehearsal, if you will." I hated Pop at that moment; he had offered up something precious to me so that this hairy-arm hero could slap it down. "Although," Bill added, "I find it delightful for a young man to show an interest in something."

"Well put," said Nguyen.

He seemed to be making an effort to win him over, but Bill returned a withering smile. "I don't mean *your* present," he said. "Your present"—he gestured at the ruin around us—"is even sorrier than his." He touched me.

We were in sight of the water now. I saw the sun melt over the lagoon, splashing pink across the launchpad and spilling through the flame trench. In the flatness of Floriday, night falls too slowly. A person has too much time to consider what the darkness might contain. Never live anywhere with too long a sunset, daughter.

In the way-back I heard Faron drum his knees. He couldn't take all this irrelevant talk of present and past. All he wanted to do was punch Bill Reade in the back of the head, and all he wanted to know was when. When would he get to fly a missile?

"No need, big boy," said Mae Reade. "Me and Bill's stunt pilots. Any flying that needs done, we'll handle it."

The Reades had attained the rank of lieutenant in the Consolidated Air Force after distinguishing themselves in the Montreal Uprising. They had taken out a Canaday parliament bunker and a Gunt convoy. But they didn't stick around to collect their medals. Instead, they stole a fighter jet at a victory flyover and flew it all the way from Ronto to Californdulia.

When they touched down at the Hollywood Airport with their baby girl asleep in the cockpit, the Reades were not met by Consolidated Enforcement but by a grinning talent agent from Bosom Entertainment. He guaranteed asylum and high-paying jobs in the movie trade.

The big Chiefs, Misters Bosom and Darling, play at rivalry. They trash-talk, firebomb each other's assets, and exalt one another's foes. Gentlemen have their own games.

For years, Bill and Mae Reade did right by Hollywood. They flew stunts in a dozen movies from *The Battle of Crystal City* to *Guts III* to *Cain Versus Abel: The Final Conflict.* They piled up enough money to buy a freestanding home in the hills, but luxury only postpones a criminal yearning.

"You steal one aircraft," said Bill, "you get the bug."

After they tried to abscond with a passenger jet, Bosom offered the Reades the same terms they'd given us. Europa or the Pens. Their daughter, having by then formed certain adolescent attachments to the Earth, reacted with characteristic noncompliance. "Sylvia gave Mr. Nguyen here a right bully beating," said Mae. "Took off his, um, hairpiece."

The victim of Sylvia's abuse pulled to a stop on a broad plain of concrete. A mound of sand and broken cement reared up beside us. "Anyway," Terry said, "nobody will be flying any day soon." Training would occupy us for nearly a year. "I do, however, have something to show you, Faron."

He said wait in the van, he wouldn't be a minute. Somewhere behind that pile of rubble a generator roared to life. Klieg lights revealed a neat rectangular pit carved into the concrete. Nguyen lifted the orange polybarrier and we crawled out to the edge of the hole. I lay on my belly looking down into a terrible darkness. It was only by my internal sense of doom that I gauged its depth. If Nguyen had tucked away a surprise at the bottom, it couldn't be good.

Faron took a less gloomy view. The minute he saw the pit, all the spite went out of him. He seized hold of my shoulders and rolled me onto my back, looked down on me, tears welling up as if he might weep into my eyes. His future was down there, his reckless future, and he hoped his only brother might share his enthusiasm. I do not know why people want so badly to make me bolder than I am.

We proceeded down to the foot of a bowed ladder where we stood atop a scaffold. As our footsteps shook the rigging, a fine spray of sand fell over our heads. I had at that time in life witnessed but one burial. It was a Jesus Lover from the peach orchards, and the last act before they stuffed his hole with calaheechee clay was to toss a handful of dust on the box. I remember how it hissed against the plywood, how the sound stuck inside me. I tried for days to dig the grit from my ears.

When Nguyen connected a pair of extension cords, we saw just how far down his excavation went. Pop steadied me, and I focused my senses on the emetic slurp of a sump pump as we continued down. Terry Nguyen would not lead us this early into danger, I thought. He drives a Darling Vanster, I thought. He knows what he is doing.

We squeezed through a network of PVC pipes and dropped a few feet to the diamond-plate steel floor. Nguyen handed out flashlights, and I saw that we stood in a hallway broad enough for a pickup. In one direction the hall ended abruptly at a wall of auto-shop shelving.

Nguyen led us the other way, to a garage door where a Pop-sized hole had been cut in the steel. He told us to take care over the debris, mostly scrap metal and fast-food clamshells, until we saw the pickup truck this hall was wide enough to hold. It was an ancient GMC so pristine it could have sat on a showroom floor. Faron ran a hand appreciatively over the hood.

The girl, Sylvia, mounted the tailgate and disappeared under a pile of white fabric. "Get down from there," her father shouted, or tried to. Something about the shape of the hall baffled any loud sounds.

Sylvia stood up. Her head and pretty neck were concealed inside a bulbous white helmet. I recognized it from the mural back in Launch Control, the stout man on the quarter moon.

"Take that shit off," Bill demanded. His anger sounded as if it were trapped in a bubble. She double-birdied her father, and that was clear enough. "Little bitch," he said. Mae hissed something I couldn't make out. The Reades were more complicated than we were, less like a family than a conspiracy.

Several yards on we reached a thick steel door. It had obviously taken some effort to penetrate, for the ceiling was scored black and a burning smell still hung in the air. Whatever strange civilization had constructed this bunker, they wanted to keep it safe from savages with axes.

On the other side of the door we entered a long tunnel hung with Tyvek. Nguyen turned over a generator and the fabric glowed white. Pale blue jumpsuits were piled up in a canvas bin. Terry said get dressed. Me and Faron stretched cotton booties over our flipper-flops, but my brother refused to wear a hairnet. He was no woman. Sylvia barked out a laugh so doggy, it made her even more beautiful to me. Umma asked Terry were we prepping for surgery.

Mae Reade spat. "Never seen a clean room before?" Her contempt for my mother was audible enough, and I hoped Umma might lay her out.

At the end of the tunnel the room opened up, big as the scramble floor at Airplane Food. "Here, friends, is the reason I halted the cruise-ship terminal project," said Terry. Four bulky objects, partly concealed by scaffolding, gleamed in the hard light. "The Constellation program. Designed and built in perfect secrecy by the last Astronomers, as the Gunts squandered the billions they had stolen from our people. The purpose of these machines is the conveyance of humans to the surface of a distant moon. Everything seven adults need to endure an eight-year journey—food, waste disposal, sleep—is contained inside."

First came the Orion Block IV, a squat cone mounted on four stumps. This would be our ride to Europa, he explained, a capsule built to pierce the Night Glass and turn circles around Earth. A connected payload stage would contain two other vehicles and a mobile home of sorts. He walked us around a buglike garbage truck with twelve wheels. The Space Exploration Vehicle. Faron was assured he would get a chance to drive her soon enough.

Suspended above the SEV hung a dull gray form that looked like an enormous plumb bob or an upside-down teardrop. Part diving bell, part drill, Nguyen said the Astronomers called this machine the Penguin. At the business end was a thermal probe powered by "advanced Stirling radioisotope generators"— nonsense words that the Reades registered with satisfaction. "My engineers tell me the Penguin can penetrate a kilometer of ice per hour. Once the saline ocean is breached, it becomes a fully functioning submersible that can support a two-person crew for up to four days."

Next he showed us the Deep-Space Habitat, a moon cabin with a rotunda as big as a grain silo. It doubled in size by deploying an inflatable loft. Nguyen handed around a stack of photos. There it was, pitched beside an arroyo way out west. With the pneumatic loft raised it looked like a tinfoil popcorn skillet, so we took to calling our future home the Popper. In the pictures, two men in those white fat suits stood around it with pickaxes. They were migrant workers, same as us, but their lean-to was considerably fancier than any the Van Zandts had ever slept in.

Mae Reade was not impressed.

"It's antiques." She rapped the Orion with her fist. It sounded solid enough to me. "You dig this coffin out of the ground and expect me and Bill to fly it? Do you have no respect for human life?"

"To answer your first question: yes. I do expect you to fly it." Nguyen was already heading back to the Tyvek tunnel. Our tour had ended. "I will point out that no one studied flying like the Astronomers. If you're saying you don't have the skills to execute our plan, we can certainly review the terms of your contract."

Umma shared her worries a different way, by sitting down on the steel floor to hug her knees. "Miss Van Zandt," Nguyen said, "this bunker has not been compromised for centuries. Not a fire ant passed through its hermetic walls until that front loader fell through. My engineers assure me this equipment, though old, is in pristine condition. And we know how to use it."

This was true. At the end of their run the Astronomers anticipated a brief exile before Gunt rule was restored. They buried the Orion until such time as it could be safely retrieved. In the case, however, that their learning did not survive the intervening age, they left behind detailed instructions. They prefabbed every piece of hardware and automated the guidance system so that even barbarians like ourselves could use their antiques. It was, as they wrote, turnkey technology.

"Sounds like a solid deal to me!" Good old Pop. He stroked my mother's hair. "See, Umma," he said. "It's space ships!" I loved my father, he meant well, but he had more spirit than brains.

"Sounds like they thought of everything but one," said Bill. "What happens when that module of yours smacks the Night Glass?"

"That—" said Terry Nguyen; he stooped down to kill the generator. The tunnel went dark. "—is what I have invited you here to discover."

7.

Back at the motor homes terry handed around sharpie pens and had us write our names in block letters on the backs of our coveralls. He said to take good care of them and they would see us through ten-plus months of training.

Pop tailored his to fit the frame of a giant. He cut slits up the sides and down the backs of the legs for his muscles, taking delight in the mutilation of a uniform that reminded him of the Cuba Pens. To Umma he said, "These might have been made in your old Pap's factory, eh?" In her jumpsuit she looked like a bundle of rods in a broke-down tent. It did not improve her disposition to recall her father.

Me and Sylvia wore our jumpsuits like juvies on turkey vulture duty. For their petty crimes these poor kids were court-ordered to collect dead birds for incineration. After a cull, they could be seen making the rounds of the Gables. Faron liked to tease them, but I felt bad. When I saw the juvies pushing

bins of vulture carcasses, all I could think of was Pop crank-
ing the handle on a sugarcane press.

Faron was the only one who resembled a proper spaceman
in his jumpsuit. "My, my, Little Brother," Sylvia said to me.
(Somehow she couldn't get that we were twins.) "Look at fly-
boy here." Sylvia could scarcely take her eyes off him, but it was
my neck her arm was slung around.

We would wear those jumpsuits every day for close to a
year, washing them infrequently in the pond, until they were
stiff with salt. Some nights, after a brutal day of training, we
even slept in them. Seven days a week we endured the same
routine: school in the morning, gym midday, and a sweaty
long afternoon of games designed to simulate conditions on
the Orion or Europa. Analogs, they were called.

In the classroom Nguyen read flatly from the stack of wire-
bound notebooks that comprised *The Constellation Flight and
Survival Manual*. We memorized every knob and toggle on
mass spectrometers, seismometers, magnetometers, micro-
scopes, and cameras. He thought it went without saying, but
we were forbidden to share any classroom learning with an out-
sider. Terry urged us to review the nondisclosure clause in our
contracts.

Bill Reade said, "Who the shit would we disclose to?"

On a tiny screen we watched ancient training videos in
which dead scholars taught us the rudiments of Astronomy,
the tangled mechanics of space flight. It was too much to learn,
and they did not deliver it slowly. They hurried through the
most arcane subjects, as if someone might arrive at any minute

to unplug their cameras. We learned how to air-clean a pressurized suit, how to mend a broken cleat, how to reconstitute tuna salad with a spigot.

This delicacy was not a salad at all but a gray paste extracted from a long-vanished ocean fish. Food was one thing that did not survive in the pit. In space we'd be growing our own. Three mornings a week we studied hydroponics and rabbit husbandry. Yams were farmed in a fibrous substrate that looked like previously owned wigs. We tried to grow water spinach in plastic tubs. But the spinach rotted and the sweet potatoes drew flies. The rabbits, in defiance of their nature, refused to multiply.

Much attention was given to the pleasures and perils of Gravity. Terry said the Astronomers described this force as a mystical fiber that binds the Wanderers to our Sun. Like desire only larger. But to hear Dr. Padma Ridley of the Jet Propulsion Laboratory talk of gravity on those ancient training videos, there was nothing magic about it. Gravity's tether, she said in her Gunt-inflected English, drew tighter as you approached a planetary body. In the vast blanks between, however, it had no claim on you. Like family, gravity was one of those things that you never miss until it's gone.

To prove it, Terry loaded us on a KC-135 cargo jet, the interior of which had been padded with stained futons. The pilot would fly to 32,000 feet and then dive straight down. For twenty-five breathless seconds we would float about, dizzy as chicken feathers from a busted duvet. It felt like the least fun bouncy castle you ever set foot in. Then, just before striking the ground, the KC would level out and gravity would grab you by the skin. I learned to position myself underneath Sylvia. I wanted to soften her fall, to be the object that drew her down.

Training mostly concerned abstinence. Doing without: food, fresh air, human-scale toilets, elbow room. Gravity wasn't the only thing we would leave behind. Europa is a world without warmth. The Reades hailed from Canaday and declared themselves impervious to cold, but having never traveled farther north than Sparkle Town, I thought ice was a substance developed by food engineers for the purpose of sno-cones.

Terry wanted to prepare us for the hardships of a distant icy world, so he took us to an abandoned skating rink. When Bill peeled the plywood off the front door I gasped. I had seen such a place only in picture books like *Blade Palace* and *Skate, Sister, Skate!* A gust of cold rolled over my feet. I smelled teen funk, sparkly vinyl flashed in the dark. We clawed our way across the rink on steel crampons. Terry flipped a switch and colored lights crawled over the ice, over our jumpsuits, over Sylvia's face like the every-flavor sno-cone kids called a suicide.

In the center of the rink Mae stood grasping the handles of a Heat Poke. This implement is a thermal cousin to the jackhammer, engineered to penetrate solid ice. As she drove in the bit, the rink began to boil and steam. The heat was so intense, it baked my legs like a campfire. Suddenly there came a thud and Umma disappeared under a multicolored fog. Pop crawled across the rink on hands and knees, rising at last with my mother slung over one shoulder. I was sure she was dying, the ice had killed her, the colored lights.

In the snack bar Pop elbowed a chip warmer onto the floor and laid her across the counter. Faron located a jug of ammonia, which Pop tipped onto a rag. "Quit it," she said, shoving him off. "I didn't pass out. I only wanted to touch the ice. I just wanted to lie down and know how it will feel."

I assumed she meant Europa. At the thinnest places its ice shield is said to be seven kilometers. It would take the Penguin, our diving bell and thermal probe, that many hours to boil through to the ocean below, seven more to resurface. Add a few hours for exploration, and at minimum we would deploy inside the Penguin for seventeen-hour tours.

To inure us to the dark, the pressure, the cramped quarters, and silence, we got a simulated taste of those deathly conditions. We were taken in pairs by fishing boat to the middle of Indian River. A two-person deepwater diving bell hung from a winch off the stern. It looked like a snakehead with a pair of glass domes for eyes, and it opened like a jaw to receive its passengers. The red-upholstered cabin made it seem hungry. Early one Saturday morning it was our turn to be swallowed. Me and Sylvia.

She stepped aboard without hesitation and slipped into the pilot's seat, but I stood at the railing, paralyzed with fear. A line of clouds was penciled across the horizon; I watched it grow into a smudge to conceal the terminal cranes at Coco Beach. The submersible rose and fell on the chop, and the cable pulsed like a guitar string.

Nguyen asked what I was waiting for, and I did not want to tell him the truth. That I was waiting to be less like me, more like Faron. Sylvia said give him a second. She offered me a sad smile. Not much in the way of reassurance, but it got me off the stern and into the cockpit beside her. As the first drops exploded on the glass, Nguyen swung the hatch closed. His features melted in the rain. The world dissolved and the cabin became all there was. To give my brain a thing to work on, I considered the plight of the raindrop, how it was torn from the water by a warm sun, how it stirred among the clouds, cold and lonesome until falling back to reunite with the happy constituency of the sea.

The submersible jolted as Terry detached the cable. Sylvia spun a dial on the dash and threw a column of switches. I heard a pump whirr behind my head as we descended.

To my mind claustrophobia is not only the fear of being buried alive. It's worse, a reminder that you are alone in life as well, an aberration surrounded by everything that is not you. The grave is a symbol of our main situation: solitude. I don't recall screaming and probably didn't. All the noise at these moments is inside my head. Sylvia's hand found mine. I shook her off and, rising on the balls of my feet, pressed my face against the glass.

Inside my chest, a second pump kept pace with the machinery. I had hyperventilated before—it is an unappealing sight— but I never did it in the presence of a cute girl. Her tough little arm hooked around my neck. She drew me in so that my head pressed against the slope of her breast. My eardrums popped, my lungs went slack.

After a while, I felt calm enough to look around. The floodlights showed a copper-colored world, mineral and dead. Is this what we would find under the ice in Europa? Would we travel so many miles only to discover the suffocated bottom of a Floriday lagoon?

Sylvia had fallen asleep. I watched her and thought this would be enough; if she was all I found on Europa, I would have everything I needed.

She choked, sputtered, and sat up so fast, she slammed her head into the edge of the dome.

"Smooth," I said.

Sylvia was not amused. "Don't watch me when I sleep."

"Okay."

"Because it makes me really upset when people do that."

"What people?"

She drew me back to her chest. It occurred to me that I knew nothing about Sylvia's life before Cape Cannibal. It occurred to me that she'd had one. For much of our seventeen hours I lay there listening to the sound of blood making its rounds through her body.

* * *

We surfaced at midnight. The skies had cleared and the Moon was up. Nguyen drove us back to the trailers, where I found Umma in bed. She said Faron had gone down with Pop to the stream hoping to catch a duck. I climbed up to the loft but was too stirred up to sleep. I was fifteen, when stirred up meant something.

After so many hours underwater, Nguyen had let us swim in the shallows of the lagoon. Even with the moonlight it was too dark for Sylvia to get a view of my clingy Y-fronts, not that she didn't try. She flung her brassiere onto the deck of the boat. "Shit was chafing my tits," she said, falling onto her back to float. "You don't care, right, Little Brother?"

I stretched out in the loft with that image emblazoned on my brain: brown Sylvia afloat on the gray lagoon. My skin was tight all over from the brackish water, but after some adjustments I slept without much effort. I wanted to dream of her; instead I found myself descending those bowlegged ladders to the bottom of the pit. I followed the bright Tyvek tunnel into the clean room, where I found the Orange Tan standing underneath the Orion capsule. He wore a shower cap and booties and looked slightly ashamed.

"You won't tell, will you?" he pleaded.

I said no, of course I wouldn't tell; but we should leave before Terry came back.

"Terry isn't coming back," said the Orange Tan. "Stay a little longer. I don't want to be left all alone down here." I woke in the night to the sound of my parents' voices. Pop whispered questions and Umma just said yes and yes. Faron had thrown one leg over me. He stank of the marsh.

* * *

Next morning Terry Nguyen surprised us with cheese danish at Launch Control. The video was about flight suit maintenance. The lights went down, and when I felt my way from the pastries to my assigned seat beside Sylvia, I found it occupied by Bill Reade. He suggested I take his seat in the front row, and I did. But I couldn't concentrate. Her father's presence behind me was an iron beam, masterful and cold. While a man talked about the daily inspection of glove gaskets, Bill placed both hands on my shoulders. He kneaded them lightly and withdrew.

That night, after we'd picnicked between the trailers, the grown-ups retired early, leaving us kids to play Uno.

"I'm his," said Sylvia, unprompted. "That's how he sees things."

Faron nodded along. He stared at the discard pile like he had something he wanted to get off his chest. I wondered if he understood what Sylvia meant.

8.

TRAINING SETTLED INTO A PATTERN THAT WAS A torment for me and tedium for the rest. School, gym, analog, repeat. Months passed, six or maybe eight. Faron and Sylvia grew more restless to embark with every passing day. The more they learned about that legendary realm beyond the Night Glass, the more they wanted to explore it firsthand. All I hoped for was to get through Gyro without making everybody take five. As for Umma, her sadness dug in to a deep quiet corner where Pop's forced sunshine could not reach.

I discovered one morning that our bathroom window had been jimmied. Faron laughed at my theory that it was burglars. It was him. He closed his pocket knife and looked over the launch tower toward Indian River. He had snuck out the previous night to swim in the lagoon. Restless, he said. I wanted to know why he had not asked me along. Instead of answering, he picked up his buttonwood branch and kept working on a toy sword.

The trailer bathroom backed up to a hairy palmetto, perfect cover for a moonlit escape. When Faron slipped out again that night, I waited half an hour and then followed. Sylvia had been acting strange ever since our dip in the lagoon. She'd cosset me, hug my neck, and chat forever about nothing—the food in the Habitat, the sex lives of rabbits, my brother. But when her father came around, she treated me so cold I thought we were no longer friends.

That night I got it in my head to draw Sylvia out of her trailer, invite her for a swim myself. If we could return to that braless moment on Indian River, maybe we'd get somewhere.

Chips of cement lay around the trailers. I collected a handful and ducked inside the mangrove. From there I could wing them unseen at Sylvia's loft window. My aim has never been especially precise. The first two skimmed the top of the Reades' trailer; a third angled off a branch and struck the wall of their master bedroom. I dropped to my belly and slid backward into the brush.

A light went on. The trailer rocked from side to side as angry feet stalked through the kitchen. When the door flew open, there was Mae Reade. She judged the trajectory and angle of impact correctly, and walked toward the mangrove where I lay hidden. Meanwhile the loft light went on, too, and I heard the muffled cursing of Bill Reade; Sylvia must have been too frightened to speak.

Mae said: "Get out here, boy." Not loud, not even mad-sounding. "Your slut is not available at the present time." Sylvia's mother knew about me, about us.

The mangrove, as mangroves do, edged a torpid stream. I frog-legged backward into the water. It occurred to me then that a pair of juvenile gators had been seen basking on the banks that very morning. I must be brave, I thought, for Sylvia's sake, and slithered deeper into the stream, hoping the moonlight wouldn't show a ripple. Something walked across my back, its legs like chopsticks, but I pressed my head into the sandy bottom to stop my lungs from bitching.

When I could hold my breath no longer, I flipped onto my back and touched my lips to the surface. How long I lay in that cemetery pose, I do not know. Pop once told me that a fair bit of love is waiting it out. He meant Umma. She had endured so many of his bad spells, his jail time. But she had tested Pop's patience as well, in ways I did not then understand.

I heard a splash, as if a gator had slipped into the water, and decided I had waited long enough. I ducked back through the brush toward the clearing, where I found the Reades' trailer all lit up. Bill sat at the picnic table, eyes fixed on the coal of a cigarillo. He, too, knew how to wait in the interest of love.

To reach our trailer without getting caught meant a long hike through the woods and up the beach. When I finally emerged beneath our bathroom window, Bill was gone and the Reades' trailer was once again dark.

In the loft my brother lay on his stomach, eyes shut but hardly sleeping. His hair was still wet. I asked if he hadn't seen Bill Reade on his way in.

"You smell like dead shit," he said, not looking at me.

* * *

The following morning the grown-ups were up and at the picnic table earlier than usual. They talked in fragments, trouble lurking in the long pauses. My name was spoken more than once. I decided I should take my lumps for last night so I left Faron dozing and crawled outside. The table was spread with decadent breakfast items, cold cuts, boiled eggs, a brownish fruit juice too syrupy for my taste. A jug of Haven Dark sat by the pitcher, and I saw that Umma was already deep into it.

Sylvia came out of her trailer and I showed her an exaggerated wince, but she didn't take the hint. I stood behind Pop, hoping his big frame would absorb the scorn Bill was about to heap on me. But I had misjudged the situation and its seriousness. This breakfast had been catered by Terry Nguyen. He loved to pack bad news in a gift basket. And this news was the worst.

"Wake up your brother," Pop told me. I was confounded. What did Faron have to do with me and Sylvia? I nearly hucked a rock at the window, then considered Bill and thought better of it.

Inside I told Faron that something was up. I helped him into his jumpsuit and peeled off a leaf that had stuck to his neck. "It's some kind of meeting outside, with the Reades and everybody." Faron looked spooked, but he walked right up behind Bill.

"Mr. Reade," he said.

"Don't smart, boy," said Bill. The Reades were awful sensitive types. "You wouldn't smart if you knew where you were headed."

This was nothing to do with me and Sylvia. It was to do with training. In four days, Mae told us, we would phase into high-intensity analog exercises. *In situ* was the figure of speech she used. I gathered from a consensus of frowns around the picnic table that this was foreign for deep shit.

Before the Constellation program was forced underground, its would-be astronauts performed analog maneuvers high in the Arctic Circle on an island called Melville. The Gunts left behind explicit directions to the base and a spiral-bound copy of their training protocol. Terry, like any other good Bosom man, was determined to run this show, fantasy or not, by the book. Months ago Nguyen's scouts had discovered the remains of a Quonset hut and a shed full of ice-mining equipment on Melville Island. If we were to thrive, even breathe, on Europa, we would need to master the ice. Drink of it, crack it, control it. Poking holes in a skating rink was an insufficient analogy for homesteading a frozen moon. So we would pass sixty days in the nearest habitat to Europa our planet could muster.

Bill Reade claimed he'd flown look-see missions in Upper Canaday. Except for the Panarctic gas fields and a few copper mines, now exhausted, he called it a valueless place, and colorless, too. (A semantic coincidence occurs to me; Copernicus took his name from that precious metal, copper.) The Gunts said white bears once ruled the land, but their numbers were greatly diminished. Bill confirmed their existence.

Those monsters are not gone, he said. "Nine feet, tail to maw," he claimed. "And whiter than snow. I shot one from my jet, and that old boy just stood up and took a swipe at the sky."

* * *

Three mornings later I woke up hugging my brother so tight, I couldn't feel my arms. Down in the master bedroom Pop was trying to coax Umma out of bed by appealing to her appetite. "He said sticky buns. Terry promised us sticky buns and fatty-meat rolls. As much as we could eat."

He zipped up her jumpsuit and fussed with her hair. Me and Faron grabbed the bags Pop had packed the night before, and together we went outside to wait.

When it came to a feed, Nguyen was a man of his word. The Vanster was filled with the delicious aromas of palm syrup and grease. We gorged ourselves as he drove to the airstrip, where the KC-135 shuddered on the tarmac. All the way from Floriday to Canaday we flew in its padded cavity. I wished I hadn't eaten so many fatty-meats. At an air base in Fort Churchill we disembarked, dry-mouthed and dizzy from the fumes, and squeezed inside a bush plane bound for Melville Island.

I had packed for my entertainment an omnibus edition of Mr. Sheldon Rosette's late-period novels, most of which I had read more than once. One work, however, I had saved for last. *Nation of Sleep* concerns the misconceived life of a Gunt senator who discovers he is not a public servant after all but a prepubescent girl living in a budget motel. Every night she snuggles in under her pink pony duvet to dream up a complete nation called the United States of America.

The bush pilot put down on a neck of land named Sabine Peninsula. To reach our lodgings, we hiked an hour over a landfill of ice and dirt. Bill was right: this was a dead world. There were no grasses to wave hello, no trees to catch the steady wind. When you spied a patch of moss, you remarked on it. Melville Island was as solemn as the Atacama Desert, minus about 130 degrees. However, Bill had been wrong on one count: the Arctic is not colorless. Its palette is every shade of miserable, like a rainbow of gloom: ice white, dull slate, a mottled red like the bloom on a frostbitten cheek.

Still, it appealed to me, the blank acreage. From the moment we touched down on the tundra, I knew I had found a home. All that space was like breathing, a long draft of wine, like laughing and not caring who heard. My bones unlocked; the unobstructed view expanded within me. Years before I arrived in the Chilly desert I knew the appeal of open country.

An icy slope bent to the gray-haired sea. Hefty as he was, Pop performed badly on this surface. Faron had to spot him the whole way down, and even in crampons the big man took a bully header. When he landed you felt the whole island bob like a floating dock.

Nguyen marched us onto a teardrop of land. Ice floes swayed on either side. Under a snowdrift we spied the zinc wall of a hut. Terry indicated a shovel and said Faron should dig his way inside to start the heater. After a few minutes my brother emerged carrying an antique Bushmaster, which he leveled at Bill Reade's belly button.

"Reach for the sky!" he said.

Cool as he could, Bill complied. I knew my brother was pranking, but I was not sure if Bill did. Also: it didn't matter. Faron's jokes often ended serious. His ironies would get all tangled up with his impulses until he was just plain mad and driven to do what he had only been kidding about. The two men drew closer till the muzzle poked Reade's gut.

"Do you suppose I have not been shot before?" he asked.

Pop tried to drive them apart but slipped and hit the ice again. Everyone laughed, even Bill.

Nguyen grabbed the gun and hurried us inside the hut. "Save your ammo for the bears."

A blue glow from snow-caked windows, the orange grin of a heater, the light inside was like permanent sunset. I could make out a small kitchen and, at one end, four pairs of bunk beds. Me and Sylvia would be sleeping in the same room, and Bill could do nothing about it. The bush pilot entered with a cheery noise—he was a whistler. He dropped a pair of crates beside the stove.

"That be all, Mr. Terry?"

"Yes, Lieutenant. See you in four weeks."

The pilot hesitated by the door. "Somebody ought to go back outside and check on that lady."

9.

High summer had begun in the arctic. the sun that set over Melville Island would descend for another three months. A single pale dusk would slowly expire until September, when night fell and stayed down till spring's gradual dawn.

Umma sat on the ice outside our hut not weeping, not complaining, only watching that intractable sunset. I suppose she reflected on endings, how infernally slow they can be. Those weeks on Melville Island were meant to prepare us for Europa, only an exercise. For our poor mother, the exercise was too credible to be endured.

The Quonset hut had grown tolerable warm. Snow melted off the windows to let in the oblique summer light. But Umma refused to come in out of the cold. Pop unrolled their sleep sacks on a bunk. He brought her a cup of tea but she would not remove her hands from that damned canvas bundle. The mug melted a hole in the snow. The water refroze around it, as well as the tea inside, while she nursed that evil baby stuffed with syringes, rubber straps, and envelopes of rock fink.

When I think on Umma today, it is this picture that replaces all the happy ones: her too-big calico dress, her laughter at some Faron foolishness, her small figure hurrying up the Dixie Hiway past the bonfires to our home.

Pop had to carry her inside the hut. She did not fight him, nor did she uncross her seated legs. He put her down, still sitting, on the bunk, and curled up around her like a cat. When dinner was over, Terry drew the muslin curtains against the sunset, signaling bedtime. I slept with my face to the wall so that Sylvia would not see the wallet I kept pressed to my mouth. As I drifted off I wondered who it was controlled our destiny: some conspiracy of Chiefs, or a lonely girl who dreamed us up from a pretty pink room.

When I awoke, in Faron's bunk, Terry was in the kitchen. I watched him perform efficient strokes with a wire brush. One by one he scrubbed and inspected an array of glass and aluminum components, laid them out on a cloth, and then assembled them into a funny little decanter. From a Mylar pouch he spooned out a precise measure of black dirt, filled the decanter with the last of our distilled water, and arranged the rig on a gas ring. In a few minutes the hut filled with a sweet mulchy odor.

Two berths over I heard Sylvia moan and shift on her springs. Not wanting her to catch me in bed with my brother, I slipped to the floor. The decanter popped and hissed like the scramble vat at Airplane Food.

"You are in for a rare treat," said Terry, not looking up from his work. I had never before seen that man chipper. It bothered me. He danced around the range in a knee-length yellow jumper, clucking two tin mugs together. With a long brown flourish he poured one for him and one for me.

I looked back at the bunks, hoping someone else might be awake. Umma slept peacefully in Pop's great arms. The collar of Sylvia's sack framed her solemn face. Mae farted.

"Coffee!" Terry exclaimed, scooping handfuls of steam into his perfect nose. He dosed the dark fluid with a squirt of sugarcane gel and watched me till I took a sip. I spat it back in the cup.

"Dead shit!"

"One of the delicious perks of archaeology," said Terry. "Occasionally you unearth a truly precious artifact." Coffee would give me strength for the job I was about to perform. "Bottoms up!"

"Job?" I said.

Would I kindly go out, he asked, and fetch a pail of water? He laughed at the accidental nursery rhyme.

"Haven't you got a spigot?"

Terry had firm ideas about how I should dress. An orange snowsuit, cinched about the waist, and a football helmet with a visor duct-taped across the face mask. When he hung a rucksack on my shoulders, I had to catch myself from falling backward. This was all part of the analog: an ad hoc space suit, a pack weighed down like an oxygen tank.

Terry removed a few large stones and said, "There!" He spun me around and kneaded my shoulders. "Like a proper astronaut!" He handed me the Heat Poke. Over my shoulder he slung the Bushmaster. "Be smart, son."

The wind that had been trying to get in all night pitched past me when he opened the door. Terry had to catch his hairpiece. I asked wouldn't it be safer to go out in teams.

Behind the hut a sled and ten-gallon drum lay under five feet of packed snow. I worked so hard digging that I didn't have the strength to pull it. As I lay down to rest on my lumpy backpack, I thought, only a minute or two.

When I opened my eyes Terry stood over me with his poisonous mug. "If you sit too long in this cold," he said, "the blood will freeze in your tubes."

He made me drink. It was still wretched. I drank some more, emptied the cup, as Terry watched, expecting a reaction. It came. I felt my spine splay out like pinfeathers, felt capable of flight, stood, and set to work. Coffee.

Terry told me to look for the blue ice. Hot springs bubbled up from cracks in the shale. Where the ice showed blue, it was warm water percolating below. I retraced our path across the scrawny peninsula, dragging the heavy sled, until I found myself back at the airstrip. Fog hung everywhere, so it was not entirely clear where the island ended and water began. Behind me the rutted seashell of the Quonset hut had vanished altogether. I was alone. An aberration. A silly orange grub afloat in a bowl of milk. If

Europa was worse than this, it might be better to die right here.

In the fog I couldn't see anything resembling blue ice. I tried a few spots, but the probe turned up only mud and shale. I dropped my bag of stones and looked around. At the far end of the runway stood a pale mound of ice and rock, a natural formation Nguyen called a salt dome. Similar features, he said, might be found on Europa.

From the summit I could look out over the island. The roof of the hut surfaced through the fog. A magic rope climbed out of the chimney pipe into the low sky. Warmth and companionship waited inside, soon as I filled the water drum.

Sure enough the salt dome was blotched with blue, frozen carbuncles. I lanced one with the Heat Poke and it slipped from my grasp into a simmering pot. I dipped in my ladle and drank. Burnt matches was what it smelled like, but clear and sweet on the tongue.

Pop met me at the door and together we rolled the heavy drum inside. My brother put up the sled while Mae dried, oiled, and broke down the Poke. I brought a mug of Terry's elixir to Sylvia's bunk. She wrinkled her nose. Her eyes cracked open. "Get that shit out of my face before I bite you."

Faron came in from the cold and stuck his frozen hands inside her sleep sack. Sylvia shrieked and fell off her bunk into my arms.

I was proud to see Pop boil the breakfast porridge in my spring water. We ate big bowls of mush with strips of dried rabbit, and the grown-ups finished off the last of the coffee.

Umma slept in, her face to the wall. When I was done, I scraped the bottom of the porridge pot into my bowl and brought it to her bunk.

"Leave her," said Pop. "Your mother just needs the rest is all. You know how travel takes it out of her." I did not know. The farthest we had ever gone was Sparkle Town to Miamy.

Umma had been looking at a bright future in textiles before Pop stepped onto her father's cutting-room floor. If she'd stayed put, she could expect to manage the sewing room in a few years' time. That noisy narrow hall would be her own chiefdom. There would be minor thrills and mishaps. A new girl would need to learn how to wind a bobbin, how to keep a straight seam, how to guide the muslin over a throat plate just so. She would have to handle crying jags, of course. Some girls would keep secret boyfriends and not be entirely honest with her, but she would give them a cup of tea and let them sob until the whistle blew. Every year she would note less and less the mocking chatter of the machines, the steady march of needle arms, until one day their noise would fill her head and she would hear nothing else. It happened sooner or later to all the girls in the sewing room. Her father would put her on bed rest till the chatter faded and she could return to work.

Umma had something to look forward to. Then along came Pop. Young, thick-armed, hair long and brightened by the Floriday sun. He called it his "Fire Mane," and the seamstresses whispered about how nice it would feel to braid it. They said the new boy smelled of oranges. He had slept in the groves, after all, and fed on nothing but fruit.

Mainly Umma couldn't believe how preposterously big he was—bigger than her father. Coylan Howard hated Pop on sight but needed the muscle. On his way from the warehouse to the cutting table, Pop always found an excuse to wheel his unwinding truck through the sewing room. He was in the late stages of a kindly patch, polite and eager to help. When Umma complained about her job at the mill, he told her she didn't have to. He wrote those words for her on a slip of pattern paper that she could pull from her apron pocket whenever she felt a need.

One afternoon a bully old cutter switched the tags on Pop's bolts just to see if the big friendly boy had a temper. While the daughter of Coylan Howard watched, Pop went at the cutter with a pair of pinking shears. That was it; she was in love. She didn't have to, and that is why Umma ran away with Pop.

* * *

Every morning on Melville Island it was someone else's job to fetch water in Terry's makeshift space suit. Pop kept Umma out of the rotation for two weeks. Give her time, he begged Terry. "She'll come around."

I told Sylvia and Faron about the salt dome, and we all agreed to keep it secret from the grown-ups. Pop and Mae worked it out somehow, but poor Bill Reade showed no talent for divining. When he banged into camp with an empty water drum, Faron made sure to greet him at the door with a kind word.

The rest of each waking day we devoted to natural inquiry. A paper journal was provided and in it we made observations on local flora and fauna, of which there were two, moss and geese. We measured precipitation, tides, and wind speeds in knots. After dinner we radioed our findings back to the empty Launch Control at Cape Cannibal. Practice.

Weeks passed and Umma scarcely left the hut. At last Terry informed Pop that she would have to go out, next morning. He expected her to participate. If she couldn't make it in Canaday, Europa would kill her.

I looked forward to sleeping in that morning, but Pop shook me awake. The Reades were asleep, and the hut was dark, but Faron was already zipping his parka. I said, "Where is Umma?"

Her bunk had been empty when Terry went to rouse her. Her parka and boots hung in the locker. Terry reported with relief that the Bushmaster was safe and sound under his bunk. The heat poke lay in its case by the door. But her canvas bundle was missing, although I did not understand why this mattered. I dressed. Faron took the rifle from Terry and we three filed out into the cold sunset morning.

The wind was light and spitting snow so fine, I thought it was sand. You could see clear to the salt dome. We walked toward the sun and I tried to imagine it right overhead. I turned the gray sea into Biscane Bay. A flying wedge of geese became pelicans. And the figure that lay on the slope of the salt dome was only a sunbather on a sand dune.

Pop was halfway there before I began to run.

Umma wore thermal long johns. The ribbed fabric pressed faint lines in the rime-frosted rock that recorded her final contortions. For a time she'd lain facing the hut, then turned her back to it. One hand she'd wedged for warmth between her thighs. Her right cheek rested on the ice. Broken veins bloomed over her nose and around her mouth. One eye was rimmed in black, open.

My father was not skilled in restoring life, only in cutting it short. He fell upon his wife as if the very mass of him might stir her blood and set her heart to pumping again. I gathered up the implements that had fallen from her canvas bundle— the syringe, the strap, the glassine envelope emptied of fink— repacked it, and slipped the bundle in my pocket. Pop lifted her off the ground, like a boy holding his puppy run down in the street. He carried Umma back to the hut when the sled would have been easier.

10.

FOR WHAT SHE DID TO HERSELF MY MOTHER HAD A cause too dark to tell. She had sorrows enough, as anyone could see. Her fugitive marriage, the father she'd abandoned; a family reduced to caged rabbits kept only for meat. But many endure worse and do not choose such a hateful exit. It must have been bad, whatever pushed her to the top of the salt dome with her plungers and her strap. Some unrevealed horror that swam in her blood. She fed just enough fink into her tubes to kill it off.

The morning we found Umma heavy snow fell over Melville Island, but a naughty wind never allowed it to land. It took two days for the bush pilot to reach us, during which time Pop did not sleep nor sit still.

Mae wrapped the body in a bedsheet. Terry and Bill made a casket from the water drum, although it took some cleverness to fold my mother inside. Knees up, head down, Umma was a tight fit. They topped her off with sea ice and pulled the drum by sled to the airstrip. Pop could have done so alone, but out of respect Terry did not ask the big man to lift his wife's body into the hold of the plane. That job was left to me and Faron.

We transferred to the cargo jet at Fort Churchill. All the way down to Cape Cannibal my father sat in back holding the water drum steady as the clumsy vessel skipped across the polar jet stream. It did not matter that the drum wasn't going anywhere. Bill had strapped it to a railing and taped down the lid. Pop rested his head on the side, listening to the melting ice shift around Umma's body.

He had lost a fight to bury our mother in the So Caroline peach field where the young couple had enjoyed their last period of unqualified happiness. Terry offered a choice of funeral arrangements: ditch her body over the Atlantic or bury her in the shallows of Broadaxe Creek on Cape Cannibal. My father was sickened by the second option, his lover's flesh picked apart by crabs, like ladies with plastic tongs at a salad bar. Bill said it would be quicker to open the cargo door and give the barrel a hard shove: we would be too high up to see the splash. But in the end, Pop needed a place to put flowers, so he agreed to lay her to rest in the creek.

Back at Cannibal Terry stored the water drum in a hydrogen cooling tank at Launch Command. He said it would take a day or so to make the arrangements. Mainly this involved finding the keys to a front loader and buying dress shoes for the ceremony. Nguyen would not contemplate a funeral without decent footwear.

While Umma awaited her burial, Vansters came and went like carpenter bees. In yellow coveralls men swarmed over the launchpad, shouting to one another on walky-talks, writing on clipboards, and generally ignoring us grieving astronauts. Typical Bosom men, busy-looking and proud. When we were on Melville Island they had raised the Orion capsule, Habitat, and Penguin from the pit and installed them in the nose of an SLS booster rocket. Now, as Faron, Sylvia, and I watched from the bleachers, the vessel made its slow crawl across the tarmac on a pair of flatcars. Rollout, a quarter-mile ride that lasted twelve hours. A hydraulic lift stood the rocket on end, and as huge gantry arms hugged it tight against the tower, Sylvia leaned on my brother. They looked at each other with eagerness, as if a whole new life awaited them.

Now and again in my trailer I would start at the sudden hiss of the fire trench snorting out clots of fog. The crew was running test firings, bringing Orion to life out there on the launchpad. In three weeks, on a Tuesday, we would perform our final fit-in and dress rehearsal. As the day approached, Sylvia's parents vanished for hours inside Launch Command to learn what all those switches and keys could do. Bill acted like the rest of us were too dense to understand, but there wasn't much to it. In their last days the Astronomers had foreseen the depths of future ignorance. They had automated the works, staging, launch, navigation, and landing. A toggle switch on a power strip, a string of code tapped on a keyboard, and away we'd go. "Plug and play" was the phrase Dr. Padma Ridley used, though it did not seem like my sort of game.

The big clock in Launch Command had ticked down to 23:08:35:00. Time sat on us. Time compressed us inside a drum and hammered tight the lid. Waiting made us wild, some with eagerness and others with fear.

* * *

But before we could go anywhere we had to bury Umma.

Pop had entered an unprecedented phase, neither kind nor cruel. He stood in our kitchenette trying out shapes with his mouth, but no expression fit a man who had sworn off grief so long ago. After his father was killed and his mother set him loose, Pop said he had forgotten how to cry. He had been left on the occasion of his sweetheart's suicide with an austere sorrow, the worst kind.

Pop would snap out of it soon enough, though, and not with a smile on his face.

I mourned in my own cowardly style. That first night back at Cape Cannibal even Sylvia could not draw me out of the trailer. After bedtime she stood under the bathroom window waiting for me to make my nightly toilet. Faron was brushing his teeth when she scratched at the glass with a palm frond. "Come out, come out," she sang. "Whoever you are." She wanted me—I was sure—but I told Faron to go in my place. I would only make Sylvia miserable. He agreed.

A few hours later I woke to my brother's heel pounding my spleen. Faron had returned and fallen into a rageful sleep. I tried to hold him down, but my brother was a twist of tendons. He yelled. He thrashed. He threw a fist that nearly knocked out the loft window. I felt him taut all over, grown large with feeling. I knew the imagined enemy on the other end of that blow, but I couldn't guess how Terry Nguyen would pay for his sins.

Not wanting a fat lip, I climbed down from the loft and slipped out of the trailer to take a walk. When I reached the moony flats of the launch area, I saw that a second, wider hole had appeared beside the first. It was shallow, only about four feet deep. The bottom was a broad white platform, the roof of the great elevator that had raised Orion to the surface.

I walked to the original opening, where we had entered the excavation for the first time so many months earlier. Below I saw the steel floor gleam in the moonlight. I eased my legs over the edge and found the top rungs of the ladder, cringing and crawling from one landing to the next until I reached the bottom. A cascade of sand followed me down, and I marveled at how quickly these secrets could be lost again. How easily I might be buried with them. How it might feel to vanish into a fairy tale with the Astronomers, a new chapter in *The Lonesome Wanderer*.

I grabbed a hard hat and stepped into the wide hallway, where the GMC truck shone warmly in my headlamp. There in the back lay the space helmet Sylvia had worn the day we met the Reades. I shivered to think of her wearing one for real.

"Faron?" The voice came from inside the pickup, dampened by the weird acoustics but clear enough.

"No," I said. "It's me. Rowan. What are you doing down here?"

Sylvia sat up as if startled and I saw a beach towel stretched over her body. "Too hot to sleep in the trailer," she said. True enough; the pit must have been ten degrees cooler.

"Your daddy know you're down here?" I don't know why I asked. At that moment I hated Bill Reade nearly as much as I did Terry. She plucked at the handle with a bare foot and the passenger door swung open. She was down to underpants, no brassiere, but it wasn't like Indian River. This was not a provocation. She wrapped the towel around her chest. I sat and she settled her calves across my legs.

She wanted to know about Umma. Where she'd come from. Who she'd been. I told her the story of Coylan Howard and the textile mill, how Pop smelled of orange zest and nearly pinked a man in half with his shears. How Umma carried me and Faron out of So Caroline to be born in a dog kennel for itinerant farmhands. She laughed at the funny parts and did not laugh at the rest, which is how I knew she understood me, as if she'd heard all my sad ridiculous stories before.

I slumped against her, pressed myself into the rough terry of her beach towel, feeling warm flesh underneath. She draped an arm over my back. I drew it to me and gave her elbow a peck. And that is how we two slept the precious last hour of night before my mother's funeral.

Morning light flooded the cab. My kidney on one side ached and both feet were pins and needles. I kissed Sylvia's sleeping face and dislodged myself from her arms. The sun streamed in through the shaft of the huge elevator, glowing in the Tyvek tunnel that led to the clean room where the Orion had slept for hundreds of years. The bay was now empty except for the blue pipes of scaffolding scattered about like picked bones. I climbed back to the surface, leaving Sylvia to the long silence of the pit. She is not your mother, Little Sylvia; she is better; Sylvia Reade is the mother of an idea; the idea is you.

Back at our trailer I was greeted by Faron's severely combed head. Raked, you might say. The tines left red streaks where he had punished his scalp. His cheeks were scrubbed bright. Even his jumpsuit looked fresh as a restaurant napkin. Instead of flipper-flops he wore the new black brogans. A second pair stood on the draining board. My feet still ache to recall them. Gifts from Nguyen, said my brother, then spit on a toe as if to polish it.

Pop, he said, had gone to fetch the body from the cooling tank.

"Umma," he clarified, as if I had not understood.

I said I thought the funeral was not until noon.

He shrugged. "Change of plans."

I had always believed Faron's strength to be inexhaustible. His strength was total and could not give, so he broke. He embraced me, pressed his face into my neck, where I could feel his mouth convulse. My brother was making words, only one of which I could identify.

"Sorry," he said. I was certain that he meant to apologize for Zoo Miamy, but there was no need. It was true; we would not be here, and Umma would not be there, had we gone to Vocationals that morning instead of stealing a tour bus. I told him to hush. It was not his fault; I had gone along willingly. There would be plenty more blame to go around when we were done.

He told me I didn't understand. "I know how much you love her," he said. He pushed me off him and patted down his hair.

I said of course; we both loved Umma very much.

He took the second pair of brogans from the counter and shoved them hard into my gut.

"Put your Jesus shoes on, little brother."

I was lacing up when the knock came, thin-fisted. Terry's knocks had come to feel like jabs, dull needles drawing blood. He wore his Bosom Industries yellows, a walky-talk strapped to the hip. Nguyen said he would not come in; there was no time. "Something has come up," he said, and he didn't have to explain what.

* * *

The first place we looked for Pop was the cooling facility. We felt through the fog to confirm the absence of Umma's body. Next we tried the Indian River pier, but came up empty again. Faron said he's running. He's getting her out of here. "He doesn't want her final resting hole to be under that rocket."

There were two roads off the cape: south past the guard station or north along the beach to the 401 and west over Indian River. The 401 made more sense, Terry said. He urged the Vanster across a culvert and onto a dirt road. Through a screen of high grass we landed on four lanes of blacktop. He stopped and looked at us. To our left the causeway squatted over the marsh grass on cement pilings.

"You'll have to take care of this," he said. "Your father would like to murder me." Nguyen was actually frightened and showed it.

Several yards ahead we spotted Pop carrying Umma's body like it weighed nothing. She was frozen in the tight ball—legs tucked, head down—that she'd made in the water drum. Only her blue feet protruded from the striped bedsheet Mae had wrapped her in. My father's feet were bare, too, blackened by the warm asphalt. Pop's Fire Mane, the tassel of hair of which he'd been so heartbreakingly proud, was chopped short. At closer range I saw that Umma's hair had come loose from its bindings. It dripped filthy icicles. Faron caught Pop by the netting of his jersey. I heard a dynamo whimper as Terry's Vanster backed away.

The tide had run out, and on either side of the road the mudflats gasped and gurgled. Crabs swayed their pincers at their doorsteps. The smell of fish rot and reed blew across the road. Everything stank of death, everything but Umma.

"Pop," I said. "You can't just take her. Terry said he won't allow it." I looked to Faron for backup. We had to pull together.

My father did not respond. Faron did. "You talk like Umma sometimes," he told me. "The old man can do as he likes."

An oak had broken through the surface of the causeway, spreading shade over the blacktop. Pop leaned the body against the tree and looked past us to the launch tower. Faron shoved me hard and I tripped over a root. "If it wasn't for you," he said, "Umma would have never signed those papers."

I asked what he meant, and I regret to say he told me. "She knew you were soft. You never were bully enough for the Gables, let alone any Cuba Pens. She only signed to save you from prison, and now look."

I did. A puddle was forming around the corpse. Umma steamed in the rising heat. The shroud softened to reveal her features, a delicate shoulder, a deerlike calf, an ear. "I didn't kill nobody," I screamed, but my voice sounded like it had in the pit, stifled and stuck inside my own head.

Pop studied his arms, blue from the inert burden he had carried across the cape. He flexed them carefully. I wanted to tell Faron he was the one to blame. He was the one hijacked a tour bus. Pop was guilty, too. Who kills a man over a jug of rum?

It was not my softness that had brought our family down; it was ill temper.

We soft ones only absorb the blows. After some fool flies into the Night Glass, we are the ones who stick around to suffer their absence. For men like Pop and Faron, the pain of life is profound but brief. Mine is like that Melville Island sunset, sorrowful and so long.

But I didn't say any of that. I was hurt, so that's what I told him. Hadn't Faron just apologized, wept on my neck? "But you just said you were sorry."

He looked at me as if I was stupid. "For Sylvia, idiot."

I didn't understand. He clarified: "Me and Sylvia," Faron said. "It's me and Sylvia, not you. Not you and anybody."

While we were fighting, Pop picked up the body again and left the shade of the tree to jump the retaining wall. He stepped into the marsh and started walking. I said we should go get him, but Faron told me Pop could take Umma wherever he wanted, walk out to sea if he wanted. Drown with her if he wanted. "A man and a woman are meant to stay together. Pop won't be nothing without Umma."

I did not see it that way, and if I stayed on the road with Faron I might have hit him, which would have ended poorly for me. I followed Pop into the marsh, but it was hard going in dress shoes. The mud wanted my brogans, so I left them behind to collect later. Barefoot was no good either. Under the pluff lay a minefield of oyster shells. I stepped carefully over the debris of a wrecked car. A bumper, hubcaps, a booster seat with a bloated dolly inside, they made a floating bridge.

Pop had already gone far ahead, showing no hesitation whatever. Even shin-deep in the muck and carrying Umma, he appeared to pick up speed. I turned back when a beer can cut my toe. Pop sat down in the water and started digging with his hands.

Faron removed his shoes and hurled them across the marsh. Pop picked up a brogan and examined it, like he had never before held such a marvelous and wretched object. Then he stuck Faron's shoe in the hole and looked back at his sons.

"I only want to sit with her a while," he shouted. "I only need—" But he didn't finish saying what it was he needed.

I said we should give Pop some privacy, although that was a joke, as crowded as he was by mosquitoes and fiddler crabs. He would come back, I said, when he was done. Faron only wished he had more shoes to throw at him. We watched Pop peel back the bedsheet and press his head to my mother's cold face, and then I dragged Faron back down the causeway.

* * *

Pop stayed out on the marsh until late afternoon. When he returned to lay the body across the picnic table, he looked worse than Umma. His legs were white with dry mud. Welts covered his face and arms. They must have been a miserable torment, but Pop refused to scratch, like he was doing a penance.

Terry located the keys to the front loader, but after a promising start it sputtered out well short of the creek where we intended to dig her grave. We couldn't leave Umma out to be torn up by turkey vultures. A mother requires proper disposal. So Mae arranged a stack of busted pallets in the Launch Control parking lot, and Bill set the pyre ablaze with a Bic and a can of lavatory disinfectant. While Umma's body snapped and dissolved in smoke, we passed around the Haven Dark and listened to Bill rattle off clichés.

When no one seemed to appreciate his eulogizing, he tried to make a joke. "Little hot for a bonfire," he said.

The effect was to remind me of the fires along the Dixie Hiway, how Umma reeked of wood smoke when she returned from the clinic to our Gables apartment. Her body, ablaze on the pallets, gave off a different sort of heat than any bonfire, like a radiant form of anger that made my skin crisp up into a shell. I understood what it felt like to be Pop, to hate so thoroughly and know the hatred would not pass until someone paid.

One flesh cooks like any other and smells much the same. Mother or rabbit. Loved one or dinner. I pressed a rag to my nose and begged the wind to shift. Mercifully it did, and then the breeze stiffened till sparks danced into the woods. We heard the first drops of rain sizzle on the hot asphalt. The fire flared up, then dimmed, as a storm raked across the cape, almost cold after the day's heat. Umma smoldered, steamed. Blue smoke spread low and thick to erase the mourners from sight.

I shouted to Pop. What do we do now? We can't just leave Umma here, half done. It wouldn't be right. Bill was quick to answer: we needed to get the body in the ground. The gators would come for her overnight, the rats. Pop stepped into the hissing coals and lifted her up. Together we followed him past the trailers to the creek in a soggy processional.

The men stripped off their coveralls and dug a shallow grave in the sandy bank. The saturated ground made for easier digging, but it took some effort to chop through the mangrove roots. While we dug, Mae and Sylvia wrapped the burnt remains of Umma's body in a fresh bedsheet and sealed her again inside the water barrel. When we were done, me and Faron covered the mound with palmetto fronds. Lacking a marker, Pop stuck his brogans upright at one end. Spaced as they were, the shoes looked as if they belonged to Umma, lying just below the surface, with her toes pointed at the sky.

The rain passed as quick as it had come on. We sat around the picnic table not saying much of consequence. It was a wake and we knew the rules. After Bill and Mae went to bed, Faron made Pop promise to try sleeping as well. Then it was just the three of us. I watched my brother's knees press against Sylvia's on the bench and wanted to drive myself between them, disgrace myself, weep, scream her name. I confess that I wanted to hurt them both, somehow. Not physically; I loved her too much to do that.

Faron grinned at her, at me, as if there was a tacit agreement that all was well among us, that I had somehow accepted Sylvia's choice. Mother's suicide should have made Faron's betrayal look petty by comparison; but if anything, one loss amplified the other.

I knew I should go inside, leave my brother to Sylvia's consolations, her knees. But I couldn't stand the thought of what they would get up to in my absence.

Terry had offered to go easy on us the following day. As the hour of our departure crept closer, I believe the man was going soft. Or perhaps he was afraid of what Pop might do to him. Either way, it meant we could sleep in the next morning. "May as well get wasted," said Sylvia.

Bill had taken the jug inside his trailer, presumably to keep Pop sober. If Sylvia went in after it, she might never come back. Faron told me to get it. I eased open the door and looked around the dim kitchenette. A little light came through the café curtains. I could see the jug on the table and Bill Reade sitting behind it.

"Looking for something?" His eyes were huge and uncaring. He despised me; I meant nothing. He smiled.

"You know, your father is going to scuttle this whole damn mission," he said. That he had come to regard Terry's trap a mission spoke to Bill's impenetrable pride. A Reade would never be a conscript.

I said I didn't know anything about that. "I just came for the rum." He slid it across the table and nodded.

"I know men like your father," he said. "Somebody always has to pay, even if justice can't do shit to make things even."

I think I asked to borrow some glasses.

"Your pa will punish Terry Nguyen for letting your mother do what she would have done anyway," he said. "Then they will kill your pa and send the lot of us down to the Cuba Pens."

"Terry would never. He needs us to fly the rocket."

"Let's just say this team, we aren't working out. Nguyen was smart enough to enlist replacements. He's been careful to hide them, but I don't miss much. They're an even uglier bunch than we are."

Bill told me he intended to go to Europa, no matter what. He would never submit to prison. His only girl would not remain on any planet with Faron Van Zandt. Bill Reade would gladly dash his family against the Night Glass before he let either of those things happen.

"Boy, you need to sit," he said. Terry had put Bill through the whole protocol at Launch Control. He knew how to key in the liftoff code; he knew how to fly the Orion, how to land it. Nguyen had been careless to put so much knowledge in one man's head.

"Plug and play," said Bill, like it was sex talk between little boys. "Here's what's going to happen: I will teach you what I know. In three weeks, you are going to sit up there in Launch Control and help us take off in that rocket: me and Mae and Sylvia."

He stood and poked around under the loft mattress. "Now I know I said you were too dense; I spoke rashly and I beg your forgiveness. Hell, even a Vocationals boy could launch that thing." I recognized the duffel bag he laid on the table. "Question is, do you know how to operate one of these?" He unzipped the bag and showed me the Bushmaster rifle.

"What if I tell?"

"Boy, I don't have to threaten you, but if it makes it easier I will." He parted the curtain. Faron and Sylvia sat side by side on the picnic table, tangling their ankles. "I will murder that brat brother of yours. That's what."

"And what happens to the rest of us?"

"Tell me, Little Brother—do you really want to go up there? It'll be eight years inside that Gunt coffin. You couldn't even stomach a few hours in the Penguin."

It was true what he said, I did not need threats; anyone could see how afraid I was. If Bill wanted Europa all to himself and his lousy family, I was willing to help.

Mae emerged from the master bedroom wearing a violet negligee. Bill told her he had everything under control, but she didn't leave.

"Me and Mae have stolen birds before," he said, taking three glasses from the cabinet above the stove and handing them to me. "I don't see how this will be any different."

11.

Dr. padma ridley taught us three rules of motion put down by a curly-wig man called Newton. Mostly you would have to be thickheaded not to have figured them out for yourself. If you push something, it will go until another thing gets in the way. If you want to move a heavy load, give it a good shove.

But there are moral mechanics to which old Newton's laws don't apply. It takes no effort at all to get a terrible sadness off the ground. Speak a few words and everyone you love will be sent away. Sign a paper and your mother dies. Tap a few digits on a keyboard and you are left lonely on the ground watching everything you care for rise up in the sky, never to come down.

I did as Bill said. He gave me no choice. Plus Faron had stolen my girl and I was petrified of eight years on the Orion. I became that man's pupil and learned how to light a fire under Terry Nguyen's rocket. When the day came, I broke into Launch Control before dawn armed with a Bushmaster rifle that I could not use. I sat down and with the slightest pressure of my fingertips stirred that great howling machine to scale the clouds and vanish. Up it roared. It hissed and departed this earth, scorching the launchpad black and subtracting from my life a great measure of love.

Newton's third law says every force has its twin, equal in intensity but headed the other way. When I pushed Orion into the sky, it pushed me back. I had to run; Terry and his goons were coming for me, and they always would be. I fled Cape Cannibal and for eight years I ducked and digressed across two continents gaining velocity until this mountain in the Chilly wastelands, high among the stars, stood in my way.

It causes me no pleasure to recount the details of my flight from Cannibal after the launch. Your father did not distinguish himself on the road. I lost teeth. I disappointed people and animals, but the end was recompense enough for so shameful a journey, because this is how I came to find you, Little Sylvia.

* * *

It was a damp, hot early morning in late May when I took off running. As one sun stood upon the ocean, a second rose behind me on the Cape, a fire I had started and now had to outpace. I crawled through creek and mangrove until the ocean appeared all broad and bright. A promising vision, the world was big enough for anyone to hide in. This, of course, was an illusion. I had places to go but no clue where to begin, so I sat on the dune and thought it was time to start crying. The sound of a Vanster engine brought me to my feet. Terry was coming; he always would be; if I didn't run, he would break me where I sat or send me down to Cuba to be with Pop.

Alongside the beach I found a road so chewed up by hurrycanes I was compelled to follow a trail of asphalt crumbs. They led me north to the crossroads of a damaged hiway, where I lay behind the sawgrass till night came and ran again.

My immediate destination was a Bosom Industries town on the far side of the lagoon. When I got there I found the off-ramp mobbed with jellyfishers, money lovers, and bums. The rocket fire was bright enough to see from miles away, and it drew a crowd across the water. I resented them for their inconsequential lives. They could drift as they pleased, from a motel bed, boat, or park bench, to loiter on an off-ramp, to smoke and boast about what a show they had seen in the sky that morning. I stood among those peasants and hated them because they owed one another nothing and had never given away what they loved.

They drew figures on the Night Glass with their greasy fingers, laughed and shouted to be heard, wagged their beards, and spat into the grass. "Backward comet," one fool kept repeating, like this was an established thing. His hands were taut with jelly stings. His buddy, drunk, reckoned it was a volcano; another man said cruise ship explosion. Some whore told me she'd seen a fireball burst against a cloud. She held my face, insisted. They were all wrong, of course, but I was in no position to set them straight. I needed to keep running.

If I could reach the Consolidated towns out west I'd be safe from Terry Nguyen. I did not know how vindictive that man could be; I knew only that I had done his project irreparable harm and that he owned a van.

Moving north, I slipped through a tan-brick subdivision that hugged the shore till I reached the head of the lagoon. A grassy point jutted into the water and on it a low adobe glowed with candlelight and pretaped choir music. I drew close to the courtyard and knelt by the gate to get a look inside. Tall tables, tall stemware, tall people. Everybody wore matching pajamas and talked with their teeth showing. Umma taught us boys to speak with our lips drawn down to save ourselves the embarrassment.

I was not so unworldly that I didn't recognize a spa when I saw one. I knew what it was this place trafficked in: nothing. Patrons paid to wait for nothing. They practiced nothing with their bodies. They pretended to sleep, which explained the pajamas. I thought: I could hide here; these were my sort of people; I had nothing either and could expect the same in the foreseeable future. Only this brand of nothing costs money, and I had nothing to pay with but two baked yams in my backpack.

Had it been Faron, he would not have hesitated at the gate. He would have bluffed his way and bullied himself right on inside. He would have hidden in a steam room till he had cooked up a plan. But I was tired and I was me. I pressed my face between the bars and shut my eyes. I heard boot heels approach over the small-bore gravel of the courtyard; the man who wore them sounded heavy and hurried. I opened my eyes to see that he was not the sort of man who wore pajamas. He wore a yellow blazer jacket and carried a pistol on his hip.

At his urging I moved along, north or maybe it was east, too scared to keep to a straight line. Finally I sat on a beach, just above the waves in a wind stiff enough to chase off the mosquitoes. Strapped to the side of my pack was a pup tent I had taken from the bed of the pickup down in the pit, but I didn't have the strength to pitch it, so I lay on the sand and asked the beach to swallow me whole. An old man wells up and blinks, never letting his tears fall, as if reserving them will keep him going. But I was still a boy and fully capable of weeping. Where my tears spilled on the sand I imagined a great sinkhole forming, like the one that exposed the Orion. I would fall in. I would plunge forever. I would go under alone as we all must at the end.

If the sand didn't want me, maybe sleep did. I shut my eyes and tried to recall how I had done it the night before, every night before, the trick of sleep. Smart Man Tolemy understood that it was cotton; we soak it with the ink of our troubled thoughts. But sleep can only absorb so much worry. That first night after the launch, I lay awake reciting the names of the animals hunted to extinction in Zoo Miamy: great big kitties painted with flames, a pony in prison stripes, a fake man in a fringe jacket. They called him the Orange Tan.

* * *

I woke in a rising surf. Foam tickled my nose, a dissolute odor that reminded me to be afraid. Up I jumped and continued at a jog along the coast. It was hard going in the sand, and I did not travel light. The Jansport pounded my rump, its straps clawed at my burnt shoulders. In addition to the yams and pup tent I carried a few paper books, a toothbrush, Pop's wallet, and Umma's canvas bundle. She had been charitable enough to leave three fat envelopes of fink rock.

I intended to dispense them medicinally. A bridge, I called it; dope would span this culvert of suffering. I measured out my cure—two a day, one at breakfast, one at dinner; take on an empty stomach—as if it was nothing more poisonous than syphilitic mercury. When Umma's leftovers gave out I intended to quit, live clean and unburdened.

I got but fifty miles up the coast before my sweet potatoes were eaten and my fink was all shot up. For analgesic I had only Pop's wallet, and my back teeth were so loose I could not get a reasonable chew on it. I fell ill with a fever; I was beat and afraid. The stiff new brogans Terry had given us for Umma's funeral killed my feet. You think you can go fugitive forever, but they don't tell you about the blisters.

My feet bled and cracked so bad that I was compelled to rest in Daytone. I needed to earn money, and that gold-tooth beach town had plenty for a boy willing to do donkey work. If there is one lesson you learn from this narrative, daughter, let it be this: don't never rest in Daytone.

I found a boarded-up tubeworm restaurant a block off the beach and let myself in. MR. JELLY CRISP is what the sign said. The thick insulated door of the walk-in cooler gave me an illusion of safety. The previous inhabitants had left behind several cartons of bread crumbs and other dry goods that had not been entirely eaten by vermin. I made my bed atop a long wire shelf where the rats could not reach me. I stayed in that vault mixing crumbs with bucket water to make porridge until I was stronger and could walk without too much pain.

After a few days I stepped out of Mr. Jelly Crisp into a bright morning feeling new, as if I had preserved my remorse inside the cooler for the rats to squabble over. With my Vocationals in mining I was able to get a seasonal job hauling sand. We trucked it from an unpopular beach to a popular one. The foreman said don't feel bad; the sand had passed back and forth twice already. I drove the front loader with a mounting sense of wrongdoing. Ghost crabs and coquinas, conchs and razor clams, they all went about their invertebrate business under the sand. What right did I have to disrupt their lives?

At night in my walk-in cooler, I lay on the shelf feeling its wire grid segment my back. I took a little fink and waited for the tar to rise about my sore feet, then waded in, up to my chest, my eyes, feeling around for Umma and Sylvia and Faron and Pop. I caught their oozy forms in the dark, but they had no density. They were lumps in a bread-crumb porridge and would dissolve too quickly in my mouth.

Daytone did me okay until the middle of October. It was breakfast time. I sat on a soy bucket picking weevils out of powdered milk, the door propped open to let in some light, when I heard voices in the dining area. Metal raked the kitchen tiles; a woman laughed. I grabbed a pair of fryer tongs for protection and closed the door. A reflexive fear stung the backs of my calves. Run, it said. Terry Nguyen was here. He had found me. I scanned the walls of the walk-in, only then realizing what a trap I had contrived for myself. The room was paneled in aluminum. A single vent on the ceiling was no bigger than my arm. I gripped the tongs and hoped Terry wouldn't look inside the cooler. But when had that man missed anything? I pictured my arrival at the Cuba Pens, the frog march down a long hall, Pop's face regarding me from the gloom of his cell: no recognition. I had left him behind.

It was not Terry Nguyen. It was two methy lesbians, come down from Jersey to winter on the Floriday sand. They wanted my accommodations. One lady was pretty and small and she waited outside while her companion rooted me out. Faron would have laughed to see how I cowered under that bully gal and her shovel. She had carried it all the way from Princeton with the express purpose of hitting somebody. It took only one blow, solid enough to knock a molar down my throat, to make me hand over my walk-in.

In Daytone I had made the mistake of sitting still. A fugitive should stay put no longer than it takes his blisters to heal.

For a week I sifted through my stool to find the tooth, but all I turned up was a missing button from my cutoffs. By then I was up the coast in Jackvill with enough cash for two nights at a lover motel. I got a funny look when I asked at the front desk for a needle, but when I showed the clerk my button, she offered to sew it on herself. I stood naked inside a broom closet till she was done. Whenever I need to remind myself of kindness, I touch that button. The clerk did her stitching well, and it has not fallen off since.

When my savings ran out I pushed inland till I reached the Ocala Forest. The Jackvill clerk had spoken of a place called Jupiter Springs. The way she talked, it sounded like a paradise. I found the water dried up and the area occupied by Seminole Indians. They lived outside Consolidated, outside Bosom, in their own Chiefdom of Fink. The Seminoles were traffickers and users both.

Their Chief went by the name Goldsmith. He started each morning grilling hoe cakes for his crew. Each day he ended with a tirade of abusive language. The Seminoles were a community bound by sporadic affection and mutual disdain. "Like Gunts," said Goldsmith with visible pride. In the still of night we would be woken by the Chief's Rejection Dance, in which he went at the hull of a Consolidated chopper with a hockey stick. I found the routine exhilarating to watch.

Goldsmith modeled his gang after an actual tribe that had run the Ocala Forest many hundreds of years before the Gunts sailed across the sea. He wore buzzard feathers on his head and no pants. His men performed what he claimed to be authentic Seminole rites. In one an initiate would be buried up to his neck in Ocala clay. The surrounding earth would be spread with dry sticks and leaves, and Goldsmith would set a circle of fire around your head. You were supposed to spit out the flames before they reached your face, but I didn't bother. When they dug me out my beard was half burned and blisters ringed my throat. Chief Goldsmith declared me the most pointless man he had ever met and he made the other Seminoles feel inadequate by comparison.

One night I could take their fellowship no longer. As Goldsmith did his Rejection Dance I slipped out of the woods with a visible wad of fink taped inside my shorts.

Outside Valdosta I trapped a raccoon to be my friend. It died in my arms.

I caught malaria picking scrap copper on the Atlanta Fill.

On the Looval Hiway I hitched alongside a girl until a medical doctor in a Vanster said he'd take her but not me.

A vessel bound for the outer solar system loops around large bodies to gather speed for its journey. Dr. Ridley called it the Veega Trajectory. The Orion would circle Venus and Earth, gathering speed from their gravitational fields, before winging off toward Europa. It is a circuitous ride full of backslides and feints, eight years long. When I fled Cannibal, I thought I was running away. Now I see I was on my own Veega, only I didn't know where all those turns would lead me.

I had my mind set on a great hole in the ground called Mammoth Cave. The Seminoles told me of a river down there called The Sticks with waters that could cure you of fink sickness, malaria, or anything. It was meant as a joke though I didn't get the funny part, and it didn't matter. I never made it to The Sticks. At a bend in the road north of Halfway, I stopped to rest. Rain had fallen all afternoon, but now it hardened into sleet. I was wet, tired, frozen, and could walk no farther when I saw a sign on the shoulder:

SCENIC OVERLOOK

I had not seen anything worth looking over for some time, so I stopped.

Here is the picture they bothered to put up a sign for: in the valley below, a hamlet hung over a stream of rust. At one end stood a yellow Vanster dealership and a Fatty Meats Express. At the other, on a rocky promontory, a picture-book castle rose in the fog, the vanity of some bygone coal baron. On its bluestone battlements stood a ping-pong table and a rabbit hutch, the whole pile flocked with sleet like a dirty sno-cone. I hoped the place was abandoned, so I jumped the guardrail and skated downhill in my brogans.

At ground level the castle was more like a ranch home with ambitions. Fatty Meat takeout boxes sailed around the moat. Mud daubers' nests hung in the gate like oriental lanterns. A burned-wood sign on the sill read CASTLE KINTEK. I called out was anybody home and was surprised to see the drawbridge stutter down.

"Come in out the cold, stranger," cried the lord of the manor, a peaceable fat man called Percy Muck. In the front hall he introduced me to his three sons, Mike, Ronnie, and Doot, a baby who giggled behind the chiffonade. Lord Muck called them his princes but to me they looked as ugly as meatballs in little wigs.

Had I known what Lord Muck wanted from me, I would not have stayed the night. He was an aspiring filmmaker who had everything he needed—a script, costumes, colored lights, three gifted child actors—everything, except a camera. Right off I was given the title of director, which meant holding a hand mixer up to my eye and shouting *action*.

That first night I studied his screenplay, a rambling narrative "of the chivalric age," when people looked everywhere for an old cup and you would kill yourself for feeling too much love. It was called *The Petit Mort of Percy* and was dedicated on the title page to "the time when a man would do anything for his family, and vice versa."

As I caught them from various angles, tracked them down the castle halls, and framed their clumsy swordplay, the four Mucks made oaths of fealty, kissed each other's rings, and rescued baby Doot from a three-headed gator. When I stopped finding them ridiculous, I grew to envy those Mucks. They were a family, and, unlike the Seminoles, it was not animosity that bound them together. It was make-believe.

I was so busy directing that weeks slipped by without my noticing. But one summer day the time came to move along. After me and Ronnie played a vigorous game of ping-pong I descended to the banquet hall for a soda. There I found Lord Muck ruminating alone on his gilded recliner. He patted one leg (Muck wore a fur-lined robe) until I sat on his knee (I was dressed in tights). Two claps and his princes hurried into the room. To general merriment he declared me an official Muck. Prince Rowan I was christened.

I looked at the three princes, dancing a circle, and saw for the first time how little family resemblance they bore to one another or to Lord Muck. He brushed my ear with his cracked lips.

Castle Kintek offered me more than shelter. Those broad battlements contained a home. Their unmade movie was a blueprint for kinship. "This old world needs to be taught the art of togetherness," Lord Muck insisted. "Without stage direction and dialogue we are but lone animals out for carrion and sex." He was not wrong, only weird, and I suppose he had been generous in letting me join his cast and crew and kin, but after what had happened to my own family, I could not be trusted with another.

The Mucks begged me not to go; little Doot wept and threw himself on the stone floor. Their masterpiece would be lost. A movie needs its director. I told them the camera was a hand mixer.

"Stay another day, my prince," Lord Muck implored me. "Stay until dawn at least. Behold: the moon burns bronze, an ill-fortuned sign."

A bit more than two years had come and gone since my escape from Cape Cannibal. In Astronomy, dates are immutable, daughter. Events in the heavens will happen when they must. I climbed down from his knee, kissed the backside of his hand, and hiked over the drawbridge, never stopping under a clear Kintek sky. As I walked I contemplated that lonely orphan Dr. Ridley called the asteroid, its tuberous heft, how it might tumble and loom as you cruised alongside. Twenty-five months into its voyage the Orion would pass the asteroid Gaspra, stealing a little more speed for the long ride ahead.

When he'd left his mother and sisters that last time, Pop hitched east from Texas to the Floriday orange groves and north to So Caroline, where he stole Umma from Coylan Howard's cut-and-sew. Throughout the year that followed I reversed Pop's trajectory, and in my mind every leg was an erasure, as if I could cover his tracks, undo myself and my family back to our beginning.

I expected distance to ease my fears, but the farther I traveled from Cape Cannibal, the more intensely I felt Terry's presence. In the lower reaches of Looseyanne I learned that a hurrycane was lashing the coast of Floriday; its outer band threw rain across the Gulf. I sheltered under a cloverleaf well aware of Smart Man Tolemy's notion, how weather bears feeling. I saw in that storm Terry Nguyen's anger blown across the land. I had stolen his rocket ship.

Even as I entered the Consolidated coast Nguyen haunted my movements. I bailed off a flash mantis farm by Leveetown when word got out that a Bosom defender had been seen idling beyond the buoys. It was night when I jumped from the pirogue. The mantis skirmished around me, flicking my ankles and popping their little flashbulbs so that a trail of light traced my path through the shallows. I was pulled out at the dock, legs bloodied and burned, sure that Terry had hooked me at last.

It was only the foreman. He told me I had two weeks left on my contract and had better return to work. Then he made me wade back through the paddy to the boat.

After my contract expired, I carried on around the Gulf. Careful not to enter Houston proper, I swung north of my pop's hometown to make some money in the Davy Crockett solvent works. Though this was a Consolidated outpost, it lay deep in Texas Bosom country. I knew better than to stay very long.

Hitching west on the Twenty Dollar Hiway, I reached Californdulia by early spring, just in time to pick fruit in the lower valleys. What Pop must have felt in the Floriday orange groves, I found in the avocado orchards outside Losang. Warmth of the sun and strong young men who camped out under the trees where rabbits were so plentiful all you needed was a brush trap and an appetite. I played cards and I swam. The harvest was not difficult. I made money and I shot fink with the boys.

By June I had earned about a million and decided to spend it all on a sightseeing hitch to Losang. Lord Muck had spoken glowingly of that golden city on the Pacific where movies have been made since the time of the Gunts. Though it was a Bosom town, the fresh air and cash had emboldened me. I felt strong and rich and reckless. Let Terry Nguyen take me in a state of contentment, I thought.

I never reached Losang. Near evening a trucker with a payload of Fanta soft drinks picked me up on the shoulder of a quiet desert route. Fanta is a charter division of Consolidated War & Jail, and I considered it safe to accept a ride from its transport crew. The cabs are always clean and warm. It is all the soda you can drink. Consolidated drivers are, by training, disinclined to ask or answer questions.

This one was different. He was going as far as San Bernadeen and filled the distance with conversation. He had been to Losang and could not recommend it. People there believe they have already arrived, he said, they've come through the desert to find the sea. They're smug and superior. Losang looks like your final destination, he explained, because you can't go any farther without getting wet.

"It is a city with no hope," he said. His advice: "Don't bother."

Boarding, as I had in flophouses and on grassy medians, I was often a target of Jesus Lovers. I could sense their soft approach well before the threefold question left their mouths. A pitying grin, the light touch, eyes that study you for the bruises made by appetite, malfeasance, or betrayal. I was plenty bruised. In the console light I could read the Fanta Trucker's intentions. He was a Jesus Lover, revving up to do me a Charity, to deliver the Gospel. I braced myself, thinking this would be my fare for a lift to Bernadeen. He removed one hand from the wheel to cup my shoulder.

"Have you met the Chief?" he asked.

When a Jesus Lover says *Chief*, he does not mean Buddy Darling or the Bosom Brothers.

I said we were acquainted.

He asked again: had I *met* him?

I insisted that I had, yes, but only in a manner of speaking.

Jesus Lovers always ask three times, like a code. If you answer yes each time, they have clearance to torment you with their Good News; but if you say no, they don't exactly let it slide either. My best advice is to run. But I was getting a free lift so I couldn't complain. Again I told the Fanta Trucker I was familiar with the story of Jesus.

He smiled and said what they always say, that Chief Jesus is no story. He flipped down his sun visor to reveal the plastic sleeve where he kept his comb. A Consolidated man must always look his best. Beside the comb he'd stuck a worried old medallion, the nipply pinup of the Jesus Lovers, the executive Chief himself. How many fink dens and tar-paper shacks had thumbtacked this image to the walls, I do not know.

He handed me the coin, allowed me to appreciate it. There was Jesus nailed to his lowercase *t*, dressed in a bath towel as if his executioners had surprised him in the shower. I always presumed he was a finkie like me. I knew he was for the downcast, the do-nothings, the weak. The *t*, I thought, must have stood for *track marks* or the lonely *terror* that grips you when the fink wears off.

"*My* man," exclaimed the driver. "*Jesus.*" Devotion is a stress on the first syllable. *Fa*nta. *Bo*som. *Je*sus. He kissed two fingers and touched the image in my hand. The trucker's rings glittered in the visor light, stacked silver bands on thumb and index.

He gave me the boilerplate—as with the Zoo Miamy spiel, I had heard this speech enough times to recite it by heart— how the Chief guarantees his return on the hot-air balloon of Jupiter to separate true from pretend. How he will reward the meek, dock the False Chiefs. Send them down to his own Cuba

Pens on Pluto. I heard again how much bread Jesus could bake and all the fish he could catch without trying.

At the mention of Jupiter I gazed through the windshield. The cluster of stars Tolemy called the Seven Sisters stood over a mountain like a question mark, as if the whole landscape were in doubt. There is no hidden meaning in starlight, but if they had anything to say, those Sisters would be calling horseshit on my Fanta trucker friend. He watched me watch the sky. I drew a breath and braced myself for paragraph two of the speech: the appeal. Would I take him inside my heart? Would I love Jesus? But the trucker surprised me by changing the subject.

"I see you like to watch the Night Glass. Do you have an interest in the antique arts of heaven?" he wanted to know.

I said nothing in reply. My interests were no business of his. I thought about Bill Reade mocking my love of history, and I hated Sylvia's father all over again for his stupid plan.

"I do," the trucker confessed. In addition to his preoccupation with Jesus, he happened to be a scholar ("largely unpaid") of the Astronomy Cults; however, his knowledge varied widely from what Dr. Ridley taught us on her training videos.

He went on at length about fortune-telling, about the invention of calendars, navigation, and the planetary deities of days past, superstitions I had learned from Umma, whose mother had preserved them from the old times. I cracked the window and listened with mounting impatience, dry wind hollowing out my ears, knowing I could correct this earnest but stupid man on every point. I wanted to tell him the future is

not "written in stars with dot-to-dot." I wanted to say the Wanderers are not the single-family homes of the gods. I wanted
to explain that the other planets are worlds not unlike our own,
that they may be inhabited by men or by snakes, by algae or
by nothing at all. They revolve, quake, burn, and freeze like
our own unoriginal Earth.

I held my tongue, closed my eyes. Perhaps he read my silence
as a judgment, but I didn't think him crazy, only misinformed.
I kept quiet for the reason that if I began to speak about the
night sky I might never stop. Three years had passed since I
hijacked that rocket. In all that time I had never once men-
tioned Astronomy.

He pointed to a spot in the southern sky above the ridge,
to the rusted bulb he rightly called Mars. Straight out of *The
Lonesome Wanderer*, he fed me the fairy tale about its Unsunk
Venice, a city riven with canals where the war god called Hell-
man poles his pirogue through channels of fire. I walled myself
off from his cracked ideas, built a classroom in my head,
switched on the monitor, and watched Dr. Padma Ridley dis-
pute every childish claim the Fanta Trucker made. Next he
spoke stupidly of the sun as a widening gap in the Night Glass
through which the ether leaks in, soon to consume us all.

"Fire next time, brother," he said, like it was contractual.
"Fire."

In my head, Dr. Ridley listened thoughtfully, then
responded: "What appears to be fiery gas is in fact plasma, a
soup of free electrons." She said it like it was holy. "The sun's

massive diameter makes it loom large in our sky. Yet even at its nearest point to Earth, the sun is a significant distance away."

"147,098,074 kilometers," I said, repeating after Ridley.

"What's that?" The Fanta Trucker gave a questioning look.

"I'm sorry?"

"You said a number."

Had I kept quiet at this moment, my future might have been very different. "147,098,074 kilometers," I said again. "It's a significant distance."

"One time I pulled a Montreal-to-Juarez," he boasted. "You want to talk significant."

"The perihelion," I said, "is the shortest distance between Earth and the sun in our elliptical orbit."

Then I was Dr. Padma Ridley, the smart ghost on the screen. I delivered in her hurried voice too many facts about the solar system, its mechanics and substance. I talked of cradles where stars are weaned, and of their messy deaths. I described the unspooling scale of everything: the moon goes around Earth, the planets around the sun, the sun around the galaxy, a whole universe projected like a movie on a vast immaterial globe. For an hour or more I spoke aloud the words I'd sworn never to repeat outside the facility and then sat back, deflated and dizzy.

"That's pretty good," said the trucker. "You know any other Astronomies?"

The man beside me was a stranger, a person I had been careless enough to trust. His cologne was suspiciously alpine, a disinfectant. The border between his shaved neck and the blond hair of his chest too tidy. The rings on his fingers too silver and plentiful.

"Only one more," I said. "There is a darkness at the middle of the galaxy, a pit into which everything fits and out of which nothing returns. I sent them there. I let them go away."

For a time the trucker focused quietly on the road, then said: "We still talking about Astronomy?"

I sank forward and pressed my head into the slatted vents until the pain became more orderly. Straight lines. I must stop talking. The hand was back on my shoulder, the Jesus Lover touch. He called me son.

"If you have sinned, you may tell me." I knew this word; it meant a crime against which there is no law. "Chief Jesus forgives. If there is sorrow in your heart, shoot it to Jesus, son. He will drink your remorse and repay you with an equal measure of peace."

Why did they talk so funny? Why was everything, I wondered, even mercy, transactional?

I told him I had said enough.

He said it was okay. Peace could be dispensed in a more general way, "if the Chief knows you are sorry." He then clutched the back of my head, driving my face harder into the vent. I struggled but the man was awful strong. Finally, after mumbling a few nonsense words, he released me.

"May peace find you," he said.

I rubbed my nose back into place. "Did you have to push so hard?" I asked.

"You must know the pain of what you done." The Fanta Trucker signaled, swerved, and looped back on an overpass. We were headed away from San Bernadeen.

"Where are we going?"

"To the mountain," said the driver. "You got to do a penance."

Hitching is mostly a safe game, but now and again you pull a sadist. I was pretty sure my number was up.

"Open your hand," he said, leaning harder on the accelerator.

I was still clutching the medallion. The bronze was damp; my fingers ached. He polished the coin on his pants leg.

"That *t*, the cross on which they nailed poor Jesus," he said, "it stands for a forgotten word."

He eased onto a county road where the range reared up in the distance. On a steep incline, he geared down and I thought it was my chance to jump. I scanned the shoulder for a soft place to land but it was all jagged rock.

"*Telescope*," he said, then spelled it for me. Even then, years before we found the observatory here at Cerro Paranal, I had a pretty good notion what that word meant. The trucker had another. "The Telescope was how them old Astronomers spied on Chief Jesus in his private home on Jupiter."

I could hear the bottles ring in the back of the truck like an alarm. I felt the cold core in my stomach expand. Fear in the tubes, said Tolemy, frost in the bones.

"Are you taking me somewhere?" I asked stupidly.

"You ought to buckle up. It's a rocky stretch ahead."

We passed a sign that read MOUNT WILSON OBSERVA-TORY HISTORICAL LANDMARK, founded by somebody the trucker drove too fast to read, in the year of 1904. A pair of whitewashed towers rose over the trees. At last he came to a stop in a dirt lot, and I thought that was it. He was about to do me. I watched him give each silver ring a quarter turn and rub his face. "Climb out," said the trucker.

We were above the timberline; there was nowhere to hide. I might have run, but I was too weak to get far. In an avocado field the night before I had cooked up my last crumbs of fink, and now the need clawed the backs of my legs, scraped out the marrow. Frost in the bones.

He went to the side of the truck and raised the roll-up door. When he reached inside I wondered what weapon he had secreted among the soda pop. He came up with a case of Fantas, pressing it on me as a gift. Then the trucker bestowed an elaborate blessing that made his ring fingers clack.

"Don't bother with Losang," he said. "You need hope, son. Only suffer for your misdeeds, tell them to the Chief, and may peace be granted unto you."

As he pulled away I stood in the dark lot, weighed down by Fantas, watching him descend without brake lights, so certain was he that no harm would come, not with his man looking down.

I looked up. The starlight was closer to me there than it had ever been.

12.

THE PARKING LOT WAS VACANT SAVE FOR A BRONZE
Wagonster all done up in comical frog stickers. I followed a
gravel path to a welcome center with a small museum. It was
after hours, the light inside small and orange, but a figure
moved among the glass cases.

When I knocked she let me in, a plump girl of about twelve
or thirteen. She stepped behind a huge ledger under a heat
lamp, shut the book, and asked what she could do for me.

I explained about my penance and the trucker who had left
me here to perform it. The girl did not respond, so I offered
her a warm Fanta from my box.

"I am diabetic," she explained. It sounded like an apology.
She produced a zippered case of syringes. I looked away.

It was just her and her mother, she said, another apology.
"Marcy started Vocationals in Bernadeen."

I said it must get lonely way up here. She stared at the heat
lamp but pointed to the pup tent buckled on my Jansport.

"You are welcome to pitch that on the grounds," she said. "It's slow this time of year."

I chose a level site beside the observatory dome with an unobstructed view of the sky and lay on my back so that I could see a slice of Milky Way between the tent flaps. The warm Fanta gnawed at my stomach. In the bottom of my pack I found a brown avocado and ate it with my fingers.

Outside I heard a woman's laughter. I was growing too finksick for sleep, so I crawled from the tent to discover the source of that cheerful sound. The laughter drew me across a footbridge to a dormitory that called itself the Monastery. It was brick and old and a fair-looking shelter for lonely contemplation. I circled the building, a pair of sodas in my back pockets, until I came to a lighted window. Inside I saw a sofa and not much else. Nobody sat there but an exceptionally large frog and he was stuffed. Somewhere I could not see, that woman kept on laughing, persistent but neither in mockery nor delight. It sounded like practice, like she struggled to learn a foreign language.

I would have shared my Fantas with anybody, even someone who did not know how to laugh, but no one appeared inside the window, just the toy frog. So I went back to my tent and tried again to fall asleep.

Not much later I was woken by vomiting, my own. The sun had not risen, though the birds discussed its shape, its brightness, its warmth at such length that I asked them to shut up. I was withdrawing. I dozed and tasted blood in my mouth the color of the sun that bobbed up among the haze. I had bitten my tongue in my sleep.

When the girl unlocked the museum at nine, I was waiting. She gave me water and a stockroom to hide in. My body turned inside out and then inverted again so that the surface felt rough and charred. I yawned so much, it made me hate my lungs. To muffle my cries, the girl cranked up an audio tour. The tape was all about the significance of Mount Wilson in the mythic landscape of the Astronomy cults. On an endless loop I heard a maddeningly sarcastic woman recite the names of the high priests who had made a pilgrimage there. Albert of Einstein, Edwin Bubble, and "Abe" Michelson, an especially daft practitioner who claimed to measure the speed of light from this very summit using compressed air, dowel rods, and mirrors.

"Light," said the voice, almost snickering. "Our ancestors imagined it to be a rapidly expanding vapor."

When the stout girl tapped on the stockroom door, I was doubled over with cramps. From what her nose did, I knew that my drawers needed rinsing. It was time to lock up for the night, snow was coming. "Did you want to stay in the Monastery?" she asked.

The laughter returned that night as I slept in a narrow cell. I rolled on the starchy sheets, slapped at imagined insects, and knew in my heart why that unseen woman laughed. She wanted, like me, to share in the joke of this world, but she didn't quite get what was so funny. When morning came, the girl knelt beside my bed. If I was fit to travel, she said, there was a job I could have in Colorado. The observatory was called Meyer-Womble, the ruins of which had recently been discovered high atop Mount Evans.

She pressed a glassine envelope into my hand. "It would mean so much to Mother," she said, "if she could keep your Fantas."

* * *

Mount Evans is a fourteener, by which they mean thousands of feet. The peak stands well above the tree line, windy and bright. And though it was summer—the third since I'd left Cape Cannibal—the days were cold. Perched at the tip-top is the wreckage of Crest House, at one time the world's highest-altitude snack bar. It stands in quiet tribute to the Gunts' reverence for foodstuffs—so says the plaque. In the gas days families would exert great effort and spare no expense motoring up the sawtooth scenic byway to sample lard-fried doughnuts and coffee at the top of the world. Before you reach Crest House, though, you pass the Meyer-Womble Observatory, a stubborn old camel of blond stone and steel with its single eye aimed considerably higher than 14,000 feet.

The climb almost killed me. I regretted instantly my decision to seek employment where there was so little oxygen. I had passed most of my life on piedmont or shoreline and was ill prepared for the impoverished air and bitter cold. At least the road was in decent shape. In its day the Mount Evans Parkway had been a level beauty, and despite centuries of ice and snow it retained stretches of smooth blacktop. One thing you can't take away from the Gunts: they knew how to spread asphalt.

Traffic is negligible at any time of year so I hiked for an hour before a hatchback Wagonster stopped to give me a lift. Inside was a family of six, sweetly put together, passing around a thermos of lemongrass tea and listening to classical. If they had been a nest of birds, they would have been chirping.

I was alone. From my haggard dress and nervous eye, I was to all appearances a person to be avoided. I shivered in a fat man's windbreaker stuffed with socks and wore two complete pairs of sweatpants, of which the outer layer bore the name of a repeat-action firearm. Why this family stopped, I do not know. Perhaps they were Jesus Lovers performing a Charity. They didn't let me ride long enough to find out.

I was put in back between two boys in car seats. When I sat down they stopped fighting and stared. I tinkered with a rip in the crotch of my outer sweats. At that time in my life I could not tolerate the nature of fabric. Weft, weave, loose threads—all too fussy for me; if a hem didn't hitch up just so, well, the whole enterprise was a shambles. I took rips personally. Resented them. I had been abusing fink three years by then. The trip from Mount Wilson had taken more than two weeks, and the glassine envelope given me by the diabetic had run out two days before.

A teen girl sat in front of me. She gawked for several minutes before I realized why. I'd been plucking the map pouch and letting it snap back, testing its elasticity. When she asked what I was doing, I explained the procedure in detail.

"Going to the observatory or the snack bar?" the mother asked. I answered yes. Her tone offended me.

"What's wrong with that man's eyes?" This was the little boy to my right talking.

"He's crying," said his brother. "Crying crying!"

"Are you saddy?"

No, I wasn't saddy. For his information, I was yawning. Uncontrollably. I had been yawning since Grand Junction. As a consequence, my eyes watered up and tears ran down my cheeks. I was not saddy in the least but thanks for asking.

Despite the oppressive heat in the wagon, I shivered. My teeth chattered and my skin felt all chickeny. I thought, *boiled chicken*, *boiled chicken*, *boiled chicken*, hoping the image might soften as it cooked.

Beside the teenage girl sat a slightly older boy, either a school friend or a child from a previous marriage. He was in the early stages of body hair, and by that I mean it grew as we traveled up the mountain. One arm was slung over the girl's headrest. It fuzzed up, thickened, like the fur of the Orange Tan but coiling and black. At that moment my ears popped from the altitude and my natural response was to blame the boy. I gave the back of his head a hurtful look and dabbed a tear from my cheek. Maybe I said something out loud.

"Okey-doke!" The wagon stopped abruptly. "How's this?"

"I thought you were going all the way up," I said to the father.

He couldn't have driven more than a quarter mile.

"We are."

I thanked them for their kindness and climbed out. Though I had been traveling through the mountains for weeks, the altitude really started hitting me there on the shoulder of the Mount Evans Parkway. It compounded the symptoms of withdrawal with an axlike headache and shortness of breath. I managed to hold it together long enough to reach the observatory.

In the front office, a manager told me she didn't expect much. The job was to drive a Vanster from the foot of the mountain to the Meyer-Womble Observatory and on up to Crest House. "Repeat on the hour." I asked had there been many applicants. She laughed. Meals and lodging were taken care of. The dormitories offered as much free bathwater as I needed. This last part was probably a comment on my hygiene.

"I have the flu," I said, thinking quickly. A space heater clicked and hummed behind the counter. I wondered if I could delay my start date by a couple of weeks to recover. I figured that was all it would take to work the residual fink from my tubes.

"Sure thing," said the manager. "Altitude can be a killer."

I could have slept in the staff dorm, but in my state I preferred the company of the mountain goats. They were plentiful, perched on every outcrop and stone wall, and did not judge. Their coin-slot eyes did not convey the snobbery you see in a lot of goats. With brilliant white coats, long sagelike faces, and beards, they looked like clerics in a cult of wool.

At the time I did a lot of vomiting and the goats didn't seem to take offense. Whenever I looked up and wiped my chin, one would be there gazing down from his high perch. Head slightly angled, hooves steady on the stone, as if to say, Hang in there, buddy. This, too, will pass.

On staff I met a pair of men who looked too thin and well preserved for their age. Gary and Ghandy lacked the same teeth I did, as if our smiles were a covert signal. They were my future. I could score from them. I was tempted, because there are only two known cures for dopesickness, dope or sickness. But I was determined to ditch fink this time for good. Maybe this was the penance the Fanta Trucker spoke of. Anyway, I reasoned, the worst of it had to be over.

After a week on Mount Evans I was so exhausted, so dry in my tubes that I could not swallow. The fatty-meat rolls in the commissary tumbled like rocks into my stomach. If I focused, I thought I could squeeze the thick, turbid blood out of my heart and into my tubes. If I didn't, I would die. So I concentrated on my heartbeat, on my flaccid lungs, on the woody pith that had replaced my muscles.

There was the easier way, and Ghandy showed it to me in the toe of his tap shoes. Ten glassine envelopes bound with a rubber band. No need to suffer, brother. I had plenty of avocado money. Umma's apparatus lay at the bottom of my pack, carried all the way from Melville Island. One afternoon I spread it out on a rock to watch the needles sparkle, held the lighter to my ear just to hear its wheel scratch the flint.

Your grandmother was handy with needles of all kinds. She had taken as much care crafting this pouch as she had sewing our yellow Vocationals uniforms. For each finkie implement she had made a separate pouch: three slots for a pair of plungers and a spoon, sleeves for the lighter and a box of needles, a zippered pocket to stash the envelopes. When I replaced the

Bic the small square of paper fell out. It had traveled farther than I had, from her father's textile mill to Miamy to Melville, and all the way up to this handsome fourteener.

I unfolded it and read Pop's handwriting: YOU DONT HAVE TO.

* * *

I didn't leave Mount Evans for nearly a year, and by the end I was a different man. Winter in the Front Range gets too cold for visitors. The road is sometimes impassable. Not that it mattered. Most runs to the base of the mountain my Vanster would come back empty. The staff at Meyer-Womble atrophied to half a dozen loners. We were the ones who had no place better to go. It was a friendless season; Gus and Ghandy hit the road at the first snow; but I no longer needed their help to fight the loneliness.

When night fell on March fourteenth I begged out of a Uno game in the dorms and took a moonlit hike all the way up to Crest House. Out on a ruined stone wall I faced the southern sky. Somewhere too far away to see, the asteroid 243 Ida streaked past between Mars and Jupiter. I had learned a few things at Cannibal about those vagrant runt worlds, and I was especially fond of Ida. Had fixed in my mind her trajectory, the dates when she and Orion would fly side by side. Was Sylvia now watching the asteroid out her window and thinking of me?

I knew where Ida was at that moment and I looked in her direction, asking her to collect all my unwanted urges and carry them off into the vacuum of space that is nothing but need. Take away the fink, I asked.

I removed Pop's wallet from my back pocket. I didn't need that either. There was very little left of it anyway. The cheap leather had been chewed to jerky, and the two halves were held together with duct tape. I said, "Good-bye, Pop," and pitched it over the edge to watch it sail into the valley. It was an act in significance if not in scale like my farewell to Umma after she left us on Melville Island. And now I was done with need. My penance had been performed and in exchange I expected peace, if not from the Chief then from Sylvia and Faron, forgiveness from Umma and Pop.

I knew then what I needed to do. I would finish my days guarding the sky, watching the night for Europa and for all the love I had lost to it.

Long ago a man as lonely as me stood on a mountain like this to gaze upon the stormy face of Jupiter. He counted its principal moons—Ganymede, Callisto, Io, and Europa. He watched them retreat behind the gas giant, saw them emerge on the other side. The lonely man saw what no one else had: that the Wandering Stars are worlds exactly like our own, with moons like our own, and a shared sun to roll around. The decent world despised him for what he knew, but after he had seen the moons of Jupiter, Galileo Galilei was not so lonely anymore.

13.

On mount evans i ditched fink. ditched pop's wallet, too. To be safe, I decided to cut ties with that mountain observatory and the whole state of Colorado altogether. Gary and Ghandy would return in the spring wearing their tap shoes and I did not need the temptation.

A more sober colleague let me know about a tour guide job at a site in the Arizone. The ruins of Lowell Observatory were legendary among the docents at Meyer-Womble. Lowell was one of the Astronomers' high and holy places, where the fiery canals of Mars were first admired, where worshippers trembled to see Strife astern her warship. Where Pluto made itself known, the Lonesome Wanderer and dwelling place of the dead, its name too terminal to be spoken. Lowell's remains, they said, were haunted with the fools of the past, dead Gunts who gazed up through broken domes still looking for their imaginary House of Death.

I hitched down to Flagstaff in decent weather. Along the way I lost another tooth in a New Mexy rest area but gained ten pounds on account of a generous taffy trucker who carried me through the canyonlands. When there was no room for me to sleep in a trucker's cab, I'd bed down on the hiway in my pup tent. When dark fell I would look for bonfires and listen for the croak of babies, two factors that told me where kindly travelers had gathered to pass the night. In the calm scoop of a median I'd open up my taffy shop, sharing sweets with children to make a positive impression. I was driven out of more than one shanty on incredible charges, but mostly people were understanding of a man traveling alone.

A crème fraîche driver let me off in downtown Flagstaff, at the loading dock of a dairy warehouse. It was the beginning of April. He gifted me a flat of crème and wished me good health. I wished I had his tidy paper hat and cheerful disposition instead. His truck and a wife to return to. But what I had was enough, a job lead and dope-free tubes.

It was a pleasant hike through juniper forest to the top of Mars Hill. I dropped my pack under a big fir where the ground sat level and soft. I didn't want to look like I had come begging.

The summit was treeless, leaving the ruins to cook in a sharp spring sun. Not much remained of the original observatory. I clambered over a stone foundation and rounded the shell of an administrative building where a sign had been hung for the Pluto Loot-o Gift Shop.

Inside a Miss Stiles looked up from her display case arrayed with iron-on patches and worthless Gunt bucks. Her wrinkled eyelids were painted green and pressed as tight as her unhappy mouth. She listened impatiently to my brief résumé: bus driver at Mount Evans, occasional groundskeeper. "They trusted me enough to let me sleep in the van." I showed her a letter of reference, although it was stained yellow with tea.

Miss Stiles waited.

I admired her selection of patches.

She looked at me like I ought to be giving her more evidence of my worth. Prove myself. The green-painted lids swelled with secret meaning. "That all you got?"

Of course not. I had plenty. But there was no point in saying I could operate an advanced Stirling radioisotope generator or pressure-clean a space suit. I told her I had driven a tour bus around the Miamy Ruins and could grow water spinach in a plastic tub.

Stiles informed me that the tour guide job had been filled. She tidied her patches.

I laid my crème fraîche on the counter, and Miss Stiles thought of something. There was day labor, she said, if I could hack it. Early mornings a crew was restoring one of the old domes. I smelled fried sweets. A radio came on in an adjoining room.

"Sure," I said. "I guess I could lay bricks."

Miss Stiles was kind enough to let me keep two jars of the crème. "You won't eat so well here," she said.

That night I camped out under the junipers, my bed soft-ened by fallen boughs. Though I had developed a hard back for gravel, it was a relief to sleep in such comfort. Miss Stiles assured me the woods would only be a stopgap till a berth opened up in the dormitory. The next morning, however, I decided to make the tent permanent. I had grown suspicious of group living, and woke up more refreshed that day than I had in years.

At five I reported to the work site. The air was thicker there than on Mount Evans, and it filled my tubes with power. Against instinct I expected something to happen. Something good. The foreman smiled, as if to say I would not be disap-pointed. You have known him all your life, your funny Uncle Chips, but I had never met an organism quite like Raoul.

When I extended my hand he jerked it vigorously, pinch-ing his waistband with the other hand. (Trousers were always falling off him for he imagined himself a much stouter man than he was.) Raoul was what the fairy tales might call a spry old fellow. Liver-spotted and lean, he hopped about like a cricket. He talked like one, too, saying more than he should after dark, and asking too many questions. He stuttered so badly, you wanted to cry.

From the looks of them, the rest of the crew had been sweat-ing away at the dome for some time before I arrived. Raoul said be an hour earlier tomorrow; they were under strict orders to vacate the site by ten, when the tour buses started rolling in. Though as far as I could tell, tourists were a rare sight on Mars Hill.

As it turned out, bricklaying was not required, which came as a relief. I had never touched a brick except in self-defense against Stairdwellers. Raoul displayed for me the finer points of a pneumatic rivet gun. "Have you ever manip-ulated a tool of this nature?" he asked. (Despite his stut-ter, Chips uses 20 percent more words than necessary.) I thought of the Heat Poke, of blue ice, and my poor lost Umma.

"No, sir," I said. "I came here to be a tour guide."

"Nothing to it." He gripped my arm.

For the next five hours I paneled the interior of the dome till my knuckles went numb from the jolts. At ten Raoul blew a whistle and waved us over to share a thermos of tea. He'd laid a pretty table in the center of the dome, six paper cups with fold-out handles. Nearby, concealed under a blue drop cloth, lay a fixed object the dimensions of a cannon, with its barrel trained on a passing cloud. Back in peach country they fired birdshot at thunderheads to make holes for the rain to spill out. When I asked Raoul what lay under the cloth, he frowned and said, "Marked for demolition," gently removing my hand from the barrel.

With a wink he pushed a milk jug in my face. A coppery smell stung my nose. Haven Dark. Considering all the poison I'd pumped through my tubes those many years since Cape Cannibal, it was remarkable no rum had passed my lips. The smell of that stuff was too reminiscent of departures, of leav-ing the Gables, of the launch, and of fleeing the Cape. Of Sylvia.

"A splash for bravery?" he asked. I did not offer my cup to be filled. I'd never had the stomach for bravery, you know. Raoul didn't force me to drink. Instead, he drew my neck under one crickety arm. It was okay, he said: "We all got here somehow."

How strange it is to be understood. How odd to be known so easily by a man I had just met. Raoul Chips knew why I behaved as I did, why I had come to Mars Hill. I said I would take my tea to go, thanked him, and hurried down to the woods for a nap.

* * *

When I woke it was late afternoon, nearing dusk. The junipers cut the slanted sunlight into knife blades. Birds were getting busy for the bugs. Ever since I had left Floriday, the sun I'd loved so well felt like a target on my head. It throbbed over my scalp as a warning to keep quiet. I was one of the few men alive who knew what the sun really was: not a lamp or a blemish on a blue glass bowl, not the widening valve that lets in the ether to end it all. Our sun is a glittering star like any other. To some distant world it is the porch light at the end of a dark road that makes a traveling man feel less alone.

Raoul sat outside my tent, a knotted onion sack on his lap. He picked drywall mud from a hairy forearm like a sparrow browsing crumbs. When I pushed through the flap, he acted surprised to see me. How was I finding my accommodations, he wanted to know. Did the work suit me? Stiles told him that

I came from Meyer-Womble Observatory; had I met a fellow there called Ghandy? What we were having, as it turned out, was not a conversation but a questionnaire. I popped a jar of crème fraîche for lunch and pushed it toward him.

"Thanks, no," said Raoul. "I brought real food."

From his onion sack he offered a past-date hoagie and a Fanta. I accepted. He fell silent, and it made me nervous to have him sitting so quiet while I ate. The spaces between my back teeth compel me to make certain modifications in chewing. I take baby bites that I soften with my tongue, jut out my chin to align the remaining molars, and grind cautiously until the paste is fine enough to swallow. It's a process and not a silent one.

Raoul listened intently, his head cocked to one side. He brushed mud from his trouser leg. He was learning my story by hearing me eat.

"Okay, then," he asked. "Why Lowell?"

I said the scenery, which made him smile. The man's teeth were almost too pretty. I wondered had he suffered at all.

"Okay," he said, folding his onion sack into a neat square. "Too soon for questions. I get it."

When I had eaten my sandwich, Raoul suggested a walk to get the digestive tubes working. He led the way uphill at a clip, past the concession and work site. Down a path of stone pavers, a promontory showed the city below, lights now beginning to come on. Raoul pointed to a second openwork dome, too small for a person to fit inside, too ornate to be

an observatory. The bronze plaque on its base had been muti-
lated by what looked like hammer blows, but this much of
the epitaph remained:

> Today what we already know is ○○○○○○○○ ○omprehension
> of another○ worl○. In a not so distant fu○○○○ we shall be
> repaid with interest and what that other w○○ld shall have
> taught us will redound to a better knowledge of our own
> and of the cos○○s of which the two form part.—*The
> Evoluti○○ of W○○○○s*, Percival Lowell

At work the next morning, I saw that the cloth had come off
the cannon. Only it didn't look like any gun I had ever seen.
A truck backed up to the site, and two guys scrapped the device
with a torch and a prybar. I ducked when they swung a winch
over the long steel barrel. This was a telescope, the very first I
had seen in person, and I knew little about them, only what
Dr. Ridley had told us.

When I asked Raoul what I could do to help, he said I'd
been "spared any complicity in this crime against human prog-
ress." One of the men secured the barrel to the winch and
slapped it.

"You have been reassigned," Raoul said to me, watching the
telescope swing over the bed of the pickup.

He gave me a grand from his own pocket and said I should
grab some breakfast at the concession stand first. It wasn't open
yet, but if I knocked hard and asked for someone named Penny,
she ought to let me in. "Unless she's in a mood." I said I knew

all about moods, and Raoul looked at me like I had no idea. Once I'd been fed, Miss Stiles would meet me at the concession to discuss my new assignment.

The concession area smelled of weed smoke. Penny's eyes were pink, and when she spoke I heard the dryness on her tongue. All she had at this hour was yesterday's boiled eggs. She lied; I could smell hoof jelly roasting on a spit in back. Penny fixed a pot of tea and served up the eggs with several packets of yellow mustard. I thought this must be a Flagstaff delicacy. Not wishing to appear unworldly, I requested extra packets.

I had just tapped egg number four on the edge of the counter when in walked Miss Stiles. She showed me a ring of keys and shut her green-painted eyes. The new tour guide, Big Doug, had already run away; if I wanted his job carting visitors around in the Mars Train, she would show me the route.

At a shed behind the main building, Stiles raised a garage door to reveal a handsome Putter golf cart. An aluminum smokestack had been welded onto the hood. Plywood planets and stars were tacked to the sides for decoration. This was the engine of the famous Mars Train. Three hay wagons made the coaches, with folding chairs nailed to the floorboards. Stiles handed me the keys and I eased the engine out of its shed, then backed up to couple the wagons.

When I pulled a chain, a cowbell clucked. In the washed-out morning light, with steam on our breath, the Mars Train took on a somewhat locomotive glory. I felt so proud of my new assignment that I pulled the chain again. Miss Stiles advised me not to overdo it.

"It ought to be realistic," she said.

The route took visitors (when we had any) from a parking lot at the base of Mars Hill up a gravel path to the observatory. I was to make four stops: the ruined library, the rebuilt dome, the Pluto Loot-o Gift Shop, and Penny's concession area, known to the public as Percy's Punchbowl. It was either busloads of Vocational kids who came because they had to or seniors who turned up for the discount lunch. Nobody made the trek to Lowell Observatory for the right reasons. Stiles said I shouldn't try too hard to educate.

"Don't overdo that neither."

I did my job diligently for three weeks, making scheduled runs to the parking lot on the half hour. Nine out of ten times I returned empty. I asked Miss Stiles if this might be a misallocation of resources. I was charging the Mars Train for nothing.

She said: "Go stand on the roof of the Punchbowl."

It sounded to me like an insult, but I did as instructed. The roof was reached by untrustworthy exterior stairs. A café table and two chairs stood on a deck of pallets. I discovered that from this aerie I could keep watch over the parking lot below. If any tourists arrived, I'd fire up the Mars Train. If they didn't, I was free to crack hard-boiled eggs on the table edge and read. I consumed so many mustard packets, my teeth and gums turned yellow.

If Penny was generous with eggs, she was lavish with her womanhood. One afternoon I was performing my daily maintenance on the Mars Train in front of the Punchbowl. While a couple of groundskeepers ate Nebula Fries inside, I scrubbed the battery contacts with a toothbrush and baking soda. I had not yet earned the right to french fries. Penny stepped outside with a cigarette and watched me while she lit up. She complimented the thoroughness of my brushing. I believe this was the first kind word she'd given me. I am embarrassed by flattery, especially from women. I explained how it was the baking soda that did most of the work.

With a screwdriver I secured a hose that had sprung loose from the coolant reservoir. Penny leaned in to admire my hands. She purred and asked when I was planning to check out her hose clamp.

Thinking she meant the mop sink in the kitchen, I asked if it had come loose.

"No," she replied. "I believe it's tight enough." People in the Arizone like to talk in code.

That evening she scratched on my tent flaps and rattled a sack full of lagers. They were pretty well skunked and the labels had peeled off, but I was glad to have a drink while Penny was around. She made me nervous.

To my eyes she was not one woman but two halves stacked on top of each other. Above the waistband her body was thin and hard, like she'd been extruded to fit inside her camisole. Her red hair she piled up high, bound so tight with a scarf that the corners of her eyes drew up. The lower half of Penny was all hips and need. She led with the pelvis, her feet scraping the ground, as if lust dragged her toward another bad decision. In this case it was me.

Penny's mismatched anatomy made sense once you saw what she was about: come-ons and insults, often in tandem. I felt both worthy of and admonished by her affection.

The clouds had settled on the San Francisco Peaks in a formation that suggested a landing. The air was scented with juniper. I was acutely aware of the cumulative stink inside my tent, the traveler's smell of blacktop runoff and sweat, but Penny settled right in. She told me I was a filthy example of manhood while her pants came off. I touched the button on my cutoffs before unfastening them, then lay down feeling the pine needles prick my back through the canvas floor like a jealous lover. Sylvia Reade was who I thought of.

Before we got started, I warned Penny that I had lost someone. "A girl," I said, clarifying.

"Why would any gal leave such a prize as you?"

"I guess I sent her away."

"Where to?"

"Jupiter."

She laughed, which hurt my feelings. I had opened up to a stranger and would pay for it. Later I would learn to speak no more than necessary during our intimate encounters, though I had not passed any time with a woman in years, and there was so much to say.

To even the score, Penny made her own confession. She had lost someone as well. A child and a man. "My baby caught the dysenteries," she said flatly. "The man couldn't tolerate my company any longer."

"Where did he go?"

She shrugged. "Jupiter?"

We joined in a hateful little laugh and then began.

Because you are my child, Sylvia, and technically Penny's as well, I will spare you the details of that night on the slopes of Mars Hill. It was welcome though not memorable. It was my first time. When we were done, she dressed and walked uphill to her dorm room, returning an hour later with a blanket and bag of toiletries. We would not be a couple as Pop and Umma had been. I withheld from her, while she continued to inflict herself on me. She mocked me and pushed me around.

Only in sleep were we proper lovers. Through the night we'd cling to each other under the sleep sack, so tight we sweated and could scarcely breathe. If one of us rolled a few inches away, the other would feel around in the dark. By morning my neck was clawed bloody, and Penny's arms were daubed with bruises.

After you came along, Little Sylvia, it was Uncle Chips who showed me how to swaddle, diaper, and compel my baby to burp. He was the one who stole formula and rash cream. Penny knew how to mother, of course she did. She loved you, Sylvia; I want to say she did. But some losses cannot be recouped.

Our nightly grappling only intensified when there were three of us in the tent. A baby seeks her mother in the dark; only natural. Penny, however, could not tolerate your wet rooting mouth, the curdled odor of sick. I would wake to find you thrashing in a corner, pull you to my chest, drift off, only to wake moments later with Penny's nails in my ribs.

By the time you read this, your mother may be gone or deceased. Maybe she has run off with a local or choked herself on Chilly ratweed.

As Penny and I went through our convulsions, I grew to love Raoul Chips. He was kind, generous, and could be charismatic to a point that was almost unnerving. In fink circles there was always a special sort of character we called a Sorcerer. This was usually an older gentleman, somewhat fallen in the social order, who got high and dispensed a lot of esoteric advice while nobody listened. He was a well-intentioned bore. A flophouse would be a poorer place without one, but you would not usually miss him when he was gone. Raoul was a Sorcerer, but he was worth listening to, because he was right.

One slow day early on, I was driving the Mars Train just for kicks. The lot was vacant, but I wanted some fresh air. At the dome Raoul hopped aboard. As usual, he began talking and would not be interrupted. The subject was telescopes, something he knew a lot about, and not just the regular Tolemy nonsense. He said the one those men scrapped had been a 24-inch Alvan Clark refracting telescope, the very device Percival Lowell used to study Venus. He'd had a few unstable ideas about cities on Mars, but by and large Lowell was a man of reason, which Raoul said was an old word for smarts.

I wondered why Raoul risked telling so much, and I asked where he'd learned it all.

"What do you know about negligees?" he said, somewhat out of nowhere.

A decade earlier he had worked for a lingerie concern in East Jersey when a floor collapsed in the basement. A common occurrence, especially where Gunt buildings had been razed and built over.

Following a sense of purpose that he described as "interplanetary," Raoul set aside the negligee he'd been stitching and went down to the cellar to explore. He picked through the rubble until his flashlight showed blue tile fifteen feet below. He says it was bra-strap elastic he tied to a standing pipe to rappel into the hole. He landed in a stairwell, which he followed down to a locked door. With a hunk of flooring he managed to break through.

Raoul found himself inside a warren of bookshelves that seemed to extend forever in all directions, an infinite underground library. He had never in his life seen so many paper books. The shadows that moved among the stacks were only rats. The carpet was boggy with sewage, and the books on the lowest shelves had rotted away. He could not say how long he remained there, in that forgotten archive, only that his flashlight had begun to flicker when he hauled up three piles of books by his trusty bra strap.

"You made lingerie?" I asked, hoping to change the subject.

He stepped forward over the coaches to show me his fingers. Though they had hung drywall for years, they were delicately tipped, drawn to pink points like pencil erasers. On them he wore stacks of silver rings, which he clicked together as he spoke.

"I did lacework," he boasted, and I did not doubt it. Raoul's mind was too elaborate for day labor. "I might show you those books one day," he said. "You would certainly find them interesting."

I stopped the Mars Train. We had reached the concession. I was hungry and hoped Penny might slip me a boiled egg. "Would I?"

"Oh, yes," said Raoul, leading the way inside. "They're all about Astronomy."

14.

BILL READE MADE ME PROMISE TO WAIT FOR HIM UNDER the bleachers. When I arrived, a pair of turkey vultures were doing a job on a dead skunk in the shade of the benches. I shooed them out and winged the carcass into the weeds by its tail. Then I sat down amid the skunk gas and rising heat for what seemed like an hour, trying not to feel trapped and knowing this was probably a test.

When Bill finally banged across the bleachers, pointedly late, he sat above me, pointedly elevated.

"Launch Control," he said flatly, strumming the ridges with his nails. "We enter separate." He arranged a small gold key between the heels of his boots. I took it. "You first."

I crept out, occasionally glancing back at Bill. He stared at the launch tower where the booster rocket now looked fit to outswim gravity. Not knowing how to walk in secrecy, I remained at a crouch and with cramping thighs waddled toward Launch Control, satisfied that my actions would not arouse suspicion.

I released the padlock that secured the door, quietly collected the chain, and entered. The sole cause of light in the control room was its red Master Clock. The transient glow clicked backward from sixteen days, eight hours, thirty-five minutes, and five seconds into a zero-hour future. I felt my way to a laminate desk and fell in behind a monitor. A few minutes passed before Bill entered the room. He climbed a few steps to the elevated platform between the glass-enclosed Bubbles. Working a crank handle, he opened the heavy green louvers. Bands of moonlight spilled across the desks.

At his beckoning, I joined Bill on the platform. He admired the distant tower and its fuming rocket; I pretended to share his enthusiasm, though my heart was rattling fast. He broke away to toggle on a power strip under a desk. Light and sound flooded a pair of computer screens. I stood behind them bathed in their preliminary blue glow. This would be my console. The placard read LAUNCH MANAGER, although someone had stuck a wad of chewing gum over the letter *a* in *launch*.

For the next hour Reade walked me through the protocol again and again. There wasn't much to it, and I got bored pretty quick. The intricacies were handled by computer circuitry and Gunt magic. I told Bill I understood, but he would not let me quit. He drilled me on that dull sequence till I could type the codes on the two separate keyboards simultaneously and without looking. He planned to be on that firecracker, he said, no matter what. He needed to know I was fit to light the fuse.

When I returned to the trailer, Pop was out cold in the wreckage of his master bedroom. Faron sat at our mini dinette asking where I had been. I said nowhere. "Just handling stuff." My brother reminded me how little stuff was left to handle. Training had ended. The rest of the job would be performed by that stupid red clock.

I suppose I wanted to hurt him. On account of Sylvia. That is why I told Faron of Bill Reade's scheme to take my brother's girl into the sky. I sat across from him and angrily peeled a yam with my thumbnail. Furiously ate it.

"Bill Reade has a plot cooking," I said. "I am in on it."

"You and Bill? Allied up? That's a snorter."

Pop undulated on the mattress like a beached seal. I said, come on, Faron; let's take a stroll.

Down by the stream I told him the particulars, how Bill had guessed at Pop's volatility, how he intended to bring his family to Europa no matter what. "He is taking Sylvia with him, so I guess that's the end of that," I said.

Faron listened with a hurt expression. "You would do that to me?" he asked.

"I would do it *for* you. So you and Pop and me don't have to fly on that thing."

"And then what's supposed to happen to me?" he asked.

"Terry would have to let you go. It wouldn't be like you did anything."

"I see. And you?"

How should I know? "Run?"

"You really know how to launch that thing?"

I shrugged. Wasn't much to it.

"Okay." He refrained from hitting me. I could see how it pained him to hold back, so I took double satisfaction in making him miserable: first for the loss of Sylvia and second because he had too much love to punish me for it.

Finally he turned to go. "You better check on Pop," he said. "I got a thing I need to do."

* * *

A boulder can't help but roll downhill, nor can a widower with impulse trouble keep from avenging his wife's death. Morning came and with it the inevitable. Pop raged out of the trailer, shouting nonsense syllables while me and Faron climbed down from sleep. He stomped across the sand and onto the blacktop, his two boys following in boxer briefs.

The Crawler Road was built to support a colossal vehicle. Each of its three lanes was as broad as the Dixie Hiway. The center was lined with fine-grained blue stone that would not make a spark. On either side was concrete slab thick enough to bear the Crawler's tractor treads. Oak and sawgrass had sprouted up through the gravel, but the concrete was impenetrable even to life, that tireless penetrator.

As big angry Pop stomped down the Crawler Road, I swear I saw the first fine cracks appear in its surface.

Terry Nguyen's Vanster approached from the opposite direction. It shivered in rising waves of heat, and I hoped the vehicle would evaporate altogether. Terry picked up speed; Pop slowed to a march.

Faron said don't worry. From the roadside he selected a broad length of oak. "Terry has sense enough not to run him down." This felt true; Pop stood taller than the Vanster and in the shoulders nearly as wide as its wheelbase. It topped out at 30 miles per hour, and that when all six batteries were juiced. He would do more damage to the vehicle than it to him.

Through the smoky windscreen I spied Nguyen's face. He did not look dismayed or alarmed, only puzzled, and mildly at that. He cocked his head like he was looking for a street sign, like he was lost but not desperately so.

Pop put his head down and charged. When he collided with the grille, the Vanster bucked back on its rear wheels. He vanished underneath like a speed bump. I heard a scrape and a crunch that was either steel or bone.

Terry drove on, still looking for that street sign.

I dived for the blackberries by the roadside but Faron seized the back of my neck and righted me. The Vanster had suffered from its encounter with Pop. The hood smoked and a pinion dragged the road. The front right tire deviated significantly from its Y-axis. Faron raised his stick and asked if I was ready. Terry worried the steering wheel. He showed his teeth and hit the brakes. I believe a moral threshold had been reached. Terry would not run down a father *and* his sons. Nguyen was not a thoroughly contemptible man, only partially. His motives, examined at a distance of eight years, were not so different from my own.

He stepped out of the van, tamping the air with his palms. Was the man actually pleading for peace? He was. Somewhere on the road behind him lay a mangled lump of paternity. Our father, the widower, mad with grief and probably dead by it as well. We had been orphaned by Terry Nguyen; the creep would make us wards of the Cuba Pens; we would come up like I Murder and meet an end just as absurd.

Faron drove the branch into Terry's windpipe and backed him up against the bent wheel. Terry's voice buzzed like a squirrel. "We can work something out," he said. "You are decent boys. I have always had faith in you."

If he was probing for humanity, I thought, he would come up dry. But a man like Terry Nguyen always expects a positive outcome. It's just a matter of performing the right actions in their proper sequence. There are only so many variables.

My brother did not feel much pity for Nguyen, but Terry had never expected that. Faron looked at the insect he had pinned against the van and he felt sorry for himself.

"Why do you always have to put us here?" It was Pop he was asking. Pop's ghost. "It isn't fair."

No answer came, so Faron withdrew the stick and drove it up into Terry's toy nose. Nguyen clawed at his face like a man trying to pull a kipper from a tin of oil. "Fuck you, Pop," said Faron. He brought the stick down on Terry's shoulder and then tossed it into the gravel. My brother walked away.

I shouted that we could not just leave, but Faron was already down the culvert and up the other side, gaining speed through the palmettos toward our trailers.

Faron had been cursing a corpse, but our father was only half as dead as he thought. Pop appeared alongside the Vanster cradling a smashed arm, his chest painted blue with axle grease. Blood pumped through a hole in his cheek.

"Give me some room," he told me, wheezing a little.

Pop pinned Terry against the van with his ragged chest. Through the gap in his cheek he blew a bloody mist across Terry's face, then dragged him around the front of the van and forced him down onto the pavement. He arranged Terry's head under the bumper a few inches in front of the bent tire.

"Put your foot on him," he told me. "Hold him still."

I stepped on Terry's chest. Pop climbed behind the wheel and asked was the man's head well situated.

I said hold up, wait, I'm not ready, and then: "Okay. Give her some gas, Pop."

If Terry said anything at all, it was the word *please*, but spoonbills can cry like a doomed man, too. The tread croaked on the cement, moving slowly. Inches separated Terry's face from the tire but Pop stretched them into a mile.

I said, "Hell. Oh, hell." Just as the rubber touched Terry's ear, I dragged him to his feet and hugged him tight. He felt warm. A fellow man. A living man. His hairpiece hung down over one ear showing a rectangle of scar tissue that suggested botched surgery. At the side of the road I gave him a shove into the blackberries. "Run," I told him.

Pop pulled forward a few feet. The blood had stopped flowing from his cheek. He looked me over: a stranger, a nuisance, something in the road. I thought, well, here it comes. He will kill me now, I thought. Beat me unconscious and leave me to die among the blackberries.

Pop's eyes turned sad. Life had not worked out the way he might have hoped. He had had expectations, I saw this for the first time; they had not been met. Then he drove off, leaving me alone on the Crawler Road.

15.

I HAVE BEEN LEFT BY MYSELF IN SOME CURIOUS PLACES. As I sat alone in the waiting room at the Flagstaff Babying Clinic, wondering how I would pay for the extraction, Penny could be heard within excoriating the nurse and me and the child inside her.

Nonfamily were forbidden in the delivery room, and until you were born I was not considered kin. I am not sure I would have watched anyway. Umma always warned us boys against standing too close to a woman's birth tubes. Pop had done so, and he wept for a month.

This was an after-hours clinic where one nurse performed the extractions, answered the phone, and counted my money under a grimy yellow light. Most of the night I was the only man in the lobby. The seats were pastel scoops so worried by backsides that I could count the bolt heads through the padding. I stood up to tour the room.

In one corner an aquarium wanted water. I peered through the algae as a single confounded eel slapped the glass with its tail. The filter gagged and sputtered. I found a plastic pitcher and filled it from the bathroom tap. After six or seven trips the tank was full and the filter ran smoothly. The eel ceased its slapping. I watched its dimpled eyes for a sign of gratitude. Instead, the animal rolled onto one side and convulsed in the suction of the intake tube.

I took a nap out of self-pity, dreamed I sat on a painful chair in a vacant waiting room, and woke to find myself no longer alone. A crowd had gathered, watching me with patient smiles. I recognized the boy from the ticket booth at Lowell, two groundskeepers, the entire cleaning crew. Our security guard paced nervously by the entrance. They formed a cordon around me, although I got the clear sense that it was not me they had come to protect.

Some invisible process had gotten under way as I slept; people don't just show up together without a reason. Beside me sat Raoul. He stared ahead at the swinging door that led to the birthing bay. Through his sparse whiskers I watched his tongue probe its cheek like it wanted out. Without speaking, he wedged an envelope between my hip and the seat.

I thought: Oh, hell. Another contract.

Inside was three million in smeary Bosom notes, enough to cover the extraction and a box of butt wipes. Raoul draped an arm over my bouncing leg and leaned in: "We are family now, Rowan." All around the waiting room bloomed the flowery grins of solidarity. "You and the baby will be well taken care of."

"Okay," I said. "I thank you."

Chief Goldsmith of the Seminole Tribe, Percy Muck of Castle Kintek, Fink Lovers, Jesus Lovers: I had, since fleeing Cape Cannibal, been offered so much family it was beginning to feel like an epidemic, a final clinging sickness that would strangle our poor world. As Smart Man Tolemy said, "The Gunts were a Cult of Togetherness, and that is how they lie down, together in a mass grave."

Swim apart or drown with the rest. Huddle like rabbits. Easier than to be plucked up by the scruff for the spit. The cordon constricted into a group hug. I wanted to run, but Doodie, the security guard, blocked the door.

A groundskeeper offered me his flask.

I refused, tried to return the money to Raoul.

"I have people on the telescope circuit," he said. "Truckers and docents, gift-shop cashiers. They told me you would come, told me where you come from." His dainty fingers danced across my jeans, the silver rings went *clickety-clack*. I shivered. The Fanta Trucker.

I thought: This is the work of Terry Nguyen. He did not need to pursue me, only to lay a trap and watch me follow its long string of lures. I was at the shark rig. The shock was imminent. In a minute Terry would step through the swinging door holding my newborn child and he would make me pay for what I stole from him on Cape Cannibal.

"Don't be afraid, Rowan," said Raoul. "This is about caring. We all got here somehow bad."

I was wrong. Terry Nguyen was not behind that door. What happened in that waiting room was my rescue from him. Sometimes around the kitchen table of a fink house—maybe the dope was hitting just right or you were just tired—a Sorcerer would reveal himself as a bona fide sage. An old fool would make sense.

Raoul tapped out a litany on my leg: "Sputnik," he said. "Mariner 4, Voyager, Hubble, Cassini, Curiosity." He spoke these names as Dr. Padma Ridley had, with the tedious reverence of a Jesus Lover. Raoul stared at the side of my head till I felt the force of his intention drill into my ear, a feathered bit. "Orion," he said.

I threw the envelope and bills scattered over the carpet.

* * *

The founder of the Lowell Observatory was a Bosstown dandy with the fussy name of Percival. He had come up in a large and well-made family, had traveled the globe and collected himself a fortune on the modest scale of the Gunts. But he was terrible lonesome. He imagined a far richer world up in the sky, heaped with treasure, lapped by seas of molten silver, and peopled by understanding women who did not make excuses.

With a rudimentary telescope he spied a network of canals, the contours of a splendid civilization, on the ruddy Wanderer Mars. Percival wanted more than life to push his own gilded barge down those thoroughfares, to dine in its opulent cafés and love its honest women. To show the world his Unsunk Venice among the stars, Percival built a powerful telescope high on a hilltop in Flagstaff, the first great observatory of Gunt America.

Lowell died on Earth. The last of his machines was that great cannon lifted onto the bed of a pickup and hauled away for scrap. Unsunk Venice was turned into a bedtime story, added to the foolishness of *The Lonesome Wanderer*. "What a fool cannot destroy, he will make absurd," Raoul always told us. He was right. But a sort of converse logic is true as well. From nonsense something real can be restored. A city can be raised from the sea.

Like Lowell before him, Raoul had climbed Mars Hill on his own unpopular mission. That forgotten library underneath Jersey contained a trove of Astronomical texts that had hitherto vanished from the Earth. They covered every manner of cosmological intrigue from the density of stars to the wingspan of galaxies. After hours Raoul descended into the stacks to learn the weight of the moon, to study the anatomy of a black hole. The ghostly energies and substances that swell our endless sky, the invisibility of the universe to us, and the insignificance of us to the universe, he read each word and carried that remnant library in his head on a pilgrimage to every Astronomical ruin in America, doing day labor to feed and board his neglected body.

He knew something few others did: that an observatory was not merely a site of religious observance, it was a machine that could see the poison rivers of Titan, the warm sea beneath the Europan crust, Lowell's Martian Canals. Along the way he quietly enlisted followers, calling them his Copernican League, the wretched of the Earth, the losers, the lonely, and the highly imaginative.

They loved him, believed in him, but there was the stink of failure about Raoul. Behind his back and with affection, they called him Moses Washington, after the clown from the comics who discovered America but was too afraid of bears to get off the boat. Raoul had the same stutter, same beard. Same doomed expression.

* * *

While Doodie calmly collected the Bosom currency off the clinic floor, Raoul told me everything. He asked would I join them. Join their club. Would I share my secret knowledge of Astronomical phenomena?

"We have chosen you, brother, for full membership in the Copernican League, Earth Chapter." Doodie replaced the envelope on my lap.

I replied that I was about to be a father. I had a good job. I didn't have time for clubs.

"I understand."

I looked at them all. The Copernicans were my people. They had mopped latrines in the Cuba Pens, picked bud by day, and slept in kennels with guard dogs. They had defiled themselves for a single tumbler of Haven Dark. They had brutalized and abandoned and had the same done to them. They were not good people, they were mine, and I wanted nothing to do with them.

"I have fallen in with unsuitable company in the past," I said, politely.

"You'll fit right in!" Raoul grinned. "Look, Rowan, I know that you have lost the ones you love. I know that some losses cannot be recouped. If you will not join us," he extended a hand, "I wish you well."

I tried again to return the envelope, but he pushed it away. The money was mine to keep. Penny was one of their own. Doodie opened the door. The Copernican League stood as a group to go.

"Do you hold meetings?" I asked. (Meetings are something I cannot abide.)

"We study," he confessed. "We talk. But mostly we search. We never stay anywhere long."

He thanked me for my time, hoped they had not been any trouble. Now, if I did not mind, there was work to be done. Once Penny finished her babying, the League had preparations to make.

"Search?" I said, catching his leg. "What for?"

"For light," he said. "Nothing more. Tolemy missed one, you know. You don't think he could tear down every telescope on Earth, do you?"

The Astronomers had been smarter than the Smart Man. They had hidden their finest arrays in backwaters. "Down in the Southern Hemisphere, in the empty nation of Chilly, the grandest telescope of all waits for us," said Raoul. "It may take us six months or a year to reach it, but the Copernicans are heading south."

Penny would join them, he was sorry to say. This news did not break my heart. I was worried about only one thing.

"You won't take the baby?" I asked.

"I don't guess she would fight you on that score. Not Penny."

Before he left, Raoul leaned over to remind me what I would be missing: the Mountains of the Moon, the Rings of Saturn, nebulae and quasars. "The icy volcanoes of Europa."

It was a pity, he said, that I would not join them.

We heard a cry from another room, and I stood with the Copernican League as the door swung open. The babying nurse entered carrying a confused bundle, red in the face from her efforts, and too beautiful to describe, you. This, I thought, is how every human meets her family, surrounded by strangers.

When I named you Sylvia, Penny did not ask why nor care. Call her what you want, she said, not knowing it was too late anyway. You had a name before you were born.

16.

Pop did not bother running. They found the Vanster where it had expired, not far from our trailers, burping steam and stinking of coolant. He had gone down to the stream to rinse his wounds. When the two Bosom men went to fetch him, they said Pop was so quiet, the ducks dipped at his feet for weeds. He had made a sling from one leg of his jumpsuit. His damp hair was finger-combed to one side, neat as he could make it.

Those same Bosom men had been assigned to guard our trailer, although nothing about them suggested they were up to the job. They were nervous, overfed, obviously third-tier. One man showed a fondness for word-search puzzles. I watched him suck on a pencil for an hour without once marking the page. I listened to his partner talk about the causal relationship between dust mites and stupidity. The links, he said, are manifest. To protect himself from mites, he slept every night on a rubber life raft. The men passed a single gun between them, an aykay that they handled like a venomous snake.

In Umma's absence it was down to me to tend Pop's injuries. I poured rum on a clean rag and taped it to his cheek. I swabbed the grease off his chest with steamy water and dish soap. Through the entire procedure Pop sat shivering on the foot of his bed, naked and docile as can be. Remarkably, his arm had not been broken but only crimped under the wheel of the Vanster. The rest of the rum I gave him for the pain and put my father to bed like he had done for me so many nights.

The following morning we were summoned to Launch Control. We entered the classroom to find strangers in our assigned seats. Three were grown men, unquestionably brothers, plump and shiny as cooked beans. Two scabby girls bickered over a bag of jerky. Two boys fought over the girls. A woman paced behind the lectern. She sucked on a cigarette, swatting away her own smoke like it was someone else's fault. Her hair was wet and she wore nothing but a one-piece bathing suit with a pattern of naked ladies. She looked annoyed, as if she had been called away from crucial sun-bathing.

"Who in tit's name are you?" demanded the woman. "And I thought we was ugly."

I said we were astronauts, but she just laughed.

Terry Nguyen entered at a bounce despite the gauze circling his head. A brown stain showed the contour of one ear.

His nose was a glossy mound of purple. He carried a binder and a Styrofoam cup half full of dark fluid.

"Lettie, if you wouldn't mind." He shooed the gal in the naked-lady swimsuit to her seat and assumed his usual place behind the lectern.

"A breach of contract," he began, reading from the binder, "may include any of the following: desertion, insubordination, failure to complete training, theft, assault, illness, or suicide." He spoke with difficulty, as if through a drinking straw. "Any member of the team found in breach may, at discretion of Program Director, be dismissed; in exceptional circumstances the entire team may be disposed of. Punishment of dismissed parties shall be determined by the Program Director and may include: a) immediate transport to the Cuba Pens, where they shall serve out their remaining sentences as outlined in section D, part 4; or b) other remedies as determined by the Program Director." He closed the binder, snorted, and spat blood in his cup.

Lettie, on her feet again, demanded to know precisely what was happening. "Exactly who is getting fired here? I for one didn't breach dogshit."

The three beans chuckled: "Here we go."

Terry apologized. Had he been entirely forthcoming? No, he had not. Did he now regret his dishonesty? Again, no. Two teams had been readied for travel to Europa. We were Team A; Lettie, the beans, and their ugly children, they were our replacements.

"Replacements?" said Lettie. "I never replaced nobody, and I am not about to start now."

"This is a high-value enterprise," said Terry. "Failsafe measures had to be implemented. I see now that I was wise to do so." He had, he said, overlooked a number of failings and indiscretions, including the "cowardly departure of Ms. Van Zandt," and "unauthorized fraternizing among conscripts."

He had gone easy, Terry said, "too lenient perhaps. But physical assault on the person of the Program Director cannot be ignored."

He stepped to the door, then paused. When he turned back to face us I saw moisture in his eyes. I hesitate to call it tears. "I tried to do everything right," he said, his voice pinched and petulant, "so that you would respect and perhaps even grow to like me. This could have been so much fun."

He was gone several minutes before Lettie piped up: "Well, shit dice and roll a seven," she said. "I guess we're still going to Jupiter." The beans slapped five.

Terry's goons appeared in the hall to escort us back to our trailers. A van, they said, would arrive the following afternoon to transport us to Hiya City. From there it was another gunboat to the Cuba Pens, where we would commence a life sentence of hard labor in the rum fields.

Bill pressed in close behind me. "That's a laugh," he whispered.

"What?"

"Terry would never let us back into the world—not even Cuba—not with what we know." His stubble scraped the back of my neck and I felt him like a virus. "Bosom has protocol, you know, cleanup agents who manage cases like us. They show up in a van and boom."

"Who shows up in a van?"

"God, you are dumb." I jerked upright as his bristles dug in. "Six a.m., boy. Tomorrow. Boot up and prepare for liftoff. I will radio Launch Control from the cockpit when it's time to reset the clock."

* * *

It was hardly necessary for the Bosom guards to sedate Pop. My failure on the Crawler Road had sapped all the fight out of him. After our father had fallen asleep, Faron called me into the bathroom.

"You swear you know how to launch that thing?" He backed into the shower stall.

"I guess."

"I been thinking," he said. "Hell if Sylvia is going away with that creep."

"What do you mean?" I said. "I have to do what Bill says. He'll kill you if I don't." Faron laughed. He liked that idea. He peeled back the vinyl paneling. The Bushmaster hung there on a pipe.

"You can do just as Bill said, brother, but me and Sylvia, we want to be in that cockpit, not Bill and Mae. All you have to do different is be at Launch Control an hour earlier. Bill says six? Have your finger on that button at five."

"I can't do that, Faron."

"I know you liked her," he said. "I know I messed up and you would rather not see us together. But think, Rowan: either way you lose her. Don't make me live without her, too. I am your brother, Rowan, and I am asking."

"Bill says they come in a van."

"What?"

"In a van, I said. Are you dumb?" I wanted to punch him right in his pretty teeth. Instead I shoved my brother so hard, he tripped backward into the stall, tearing down the curtain as he fell. I knelt and spat in his face: "Bill said it was a protocol. Cleanup agents. A van. Terry means to kill us all tomorrow."

Pop moaned. I looked to the master bedroom as he swung a heavy arm at the nightstand. The resin lamp thudded on the floor and he resumed snoring. Faron got to his feet.

"Terry won't kill shit. Not me anyways." He elbowed past me into the kitchenette. "Or you if I have anything to say. When that rocket takes off, he's going to be too busy pulling out his hair to see you slip off into the woods. You'll be half-way up the coast before Terry even knows you're gone."

"Great. Then come with me," I said. "Let the Reades take off if they want to so bad. You and me will run. We ran before, Faron."

"Look how that worked out."

My brother smiled. It wasn't just Sylvia. He wanted to be on that rocket for his own reasons, for Faron reasons. He thought he would go to Europa, set himself up with a new life.

"There is nothing good waiting for me down here," he said. "Nothing."

17.

It was summer in the Arizone, early September, when the Copernican League, weighed down with tents and cookstoves, departed fourteen strong from the Lowell Observatory. The telescope Raoul set his sights on lay five thousand miles south, on a hilltop called Cerro Paranal in the Atacama Desert. The Very Large Telescope was, he promised us, the final unmolested, nonransacked array on Earth, with four 8.2-meter optical telescopes and a warren of mirrored tunnels that siphon the starlight into an underground chamber.

By morning we made the gravel city of Two-Son, where we boarded a train bound for Mexy Town, spreading out across six different coaches to avoid suspicion. Raoul forbade open talk with our fellow Copernicans; instead messages were conveyed on slips of paper, which we inserted in the folds of sticky buns. These were for sale in the café car, wrapped in plastic, and when one was delivered you had to eat it right away, along with the note. Some mornings as many as fourteen buns appeared on my overhead luggage rack.

Our leader's paranoia had lain dormant on Mars Hill. Now it emerged like a hermit crab from its seashell, impotently snapping at every imagined threat. His worries were not entirely unjustified. What I had seen and done at Cape Cannibal made me an asset. I knew more about the dull mechanics of Astronomy than just about anyone alive. But knowing can make you a liability. In me, the Copernican League harbored a saboteur, a man on the lam from certain incarceration, a fugitive in possession of proprietary corporate secrets, and therefore a person of interest to either Bosom Enterprises or its rival.

For my part, I felt safer in the company of the Copernicans. Raoul was widely regarded, if at all, as an idiot. Still, I kept a blade in my sock, M-80s in a paper bag. If there was any trouble, I intended to slash and bang my way off that Mexy locomotive. To protect your baby eardrums, I kept two small wads of cotton in my breast pocket. I would tape shut your eyes if need be to preserve you from the meanness in this world.

Just below the border our train lurched through the toiletry and detergent hub of Nogolly. Glass towers swayed on either side of the railbed, throwing a silvery glow of commerce over the train. I cracked the transom window to let in the famously perfumed air of the Scented Valley. Breathed deep, because people said you could take that sweetness with you for the rest of your life. That the vapors could cure pleurisy and lameness, self-doubt or sloth. We chugged slow through zones of fragrance: Minty-Fresh breath, Citrus shampoo, Sanitary Pine like the cleanest motel restroom you ever relieved yourself in.

A responsible father would have hopped off the train right there. He would have orphaned his baby girl in the lobby of one of those bright buildings, snug on a white leather sofa to be discovered by a hygienic female CEO. To be raised, as the saying goes, rich and right.

We hissed to a stop beside a frosted-glass depot. On the platform opposite, a crowd waited for their own train. Women and men, they shared a fellowship of good grooming. They smiled at one another without speaking, as if the object of their pleasure were too obvious to mention. Suit jackets slung over one shoulder; hosiery scrubbed white. Despite the oppressive heat there wouldn't be a single sweat stain on those pricey fabrics. You held my pinkie finger. Your diaper had wanted changing since we crossed the border.

Had I skipped Faron's invitation to Zoo Miamy that day, I might have offered you a decent life, Little Sylvia. No Scented Valley, mind you, only regular. But regular was not the sort of life Terry Nguyen stuck me with. At least, I thought, you won't grow up a fool. Look at those people on the platform, I said, wagging your damp fist with my pinkie, "every one a fool and they don't even know it."

Early the second morning we entered the badlands of Upper Mexy. Most of the fink I had used had been cooked up on that sorry stretch. I looked out on the sun-red desert and saw an anti-heart, an organ that pumped black tar. When you are old enough I will give your grandmother's canvas bundle to you so that you may burn it.

Another night arrived, still on the train. You cried. You slept. You gazed up at my face, at the sky outside our window. Orion's Belt. The Sierra Mama. Mountains move slow, I sang, stars hardly at all. I named the ones I knew, and your feet kicked at the sound of my voice. I would find a hole in the Night Glass where I could lift you through. I would follow you up and stamp on the sky till it shattered into pieces across the Earth.

Morning returned. You were hungry. I fed you formula thinned with water from the lavatory. Your mother did not ask to hold you, and I was glad she kept her distance. You were all mine, Sylvia.

The whole way to Mexy Town, Raoul sulked in the bar car, inserting one frightened message after another into the sticky buns. Eventually his gloom alienated the Lowell cleaning staff. By the time we reached the capital, our number had been reduced to eleven. He decided it was rail travel that was killing morale. No more trains.

Penny asked around and found a previously owned school bus for sale. While the others waited in the zocalo, me and Raoul met the seller out back of a mattress wholesaler. She was a grandmother of almost perfectly spherical proportions but fit. The bus less so, though Raoul judged it sufficient. After she showed us under the hood, the old woman popped a compartment beneath the dash. Inside she indicated us a bullwhip with beads on the stinger end and said you never knew. Raoul nodded.

"Yes," I said. "It's going to be a long ride."

"You going out looking for schools?" the lady wanted to know. One side of the bus was painted with the words ROMA NORTE VOCATIONALS.

I thought it was a joke, but she did not laugh. "No," I replied. "Just regular sightseeing."

"Because you could pull up in front of any elementary school in Mexy," she said, "pick up some kids, and nobody would bat an eyeball." Her brow wrinkled and she stuck out her bottom lip. I guessed she was right about that, although I said we didn't plan to give rides to children. "Okay," she said with a dirty laugh. "You got it, man!"

She wondered how we were set for lodging. Her husband was a licensed travel agent, and he would be happy to make some calls. Raoul told her we planned to camp out. "Ha!" Her eyes narrowed. "He's the smart one. Keep to the shadows until you find the right school. Then: *ding, ding, ding, ding, ding*!" She pinched the air with each ding like it was something actual.

The conversation was making me uneasy. Night was falling. I told Raoul we'd better hit the road. The woman rocked back and forth for a minute, such that I thought she might roll away. "Tell you what," she said. "You don't need to pitch a tent. Help me remove these seats."

Thirty minutes later, we were bouncing back to the zocalo with four showroom model futons lining the back of the bus. I told Raoul about the cargo plane with its padded fuselage. He said he'd experienced microgravity himself, prior to birth.

When we arrived at the zocalo, Penny had already bought supplies. Thirty jugs of filtered water, stacks of fresh tortillas, knots of string cheese, peanut butter, and a burrito-sized wad of cannabis. From a $99 store she'd bought a hundred tube socks and a box of what were termed "bulk undergarments." Tyvek disposables for institutional use. They came in hospital blue and could be sized to fit with adhesive strips.

By the time we reached Salvador it was so hot those underpants were all we could stand to wear. The sun lit up our bus like a toaster oven, so we drove by night, windows wide, as we sweated out the residue of peanut butter and string cheese. People are wrong about the Scented Valley; you can't take that sweetness with you.

For the sake of your health, Penny agreed to blow her weed smoke out the back window. Now there was a bully sight: plump-bottom Penny, breasts shiny with sweat, her Tyvek undershorts rustling in the wind, and a trail of smoke flowing behind the school bus. I thought of the contrail beneath the rocket, of the clear view from Launch Control, and in my memory worked backward to tell you stories of Umma and Pop, the mill and the orange groves. While I brushed damp strands from your cheek I whispered about a naked swim in Indian River and a night in the cab of a pickup way down in the cool of the pit.

* * *

Next came the desert. From Dr. Padma Ridley I had learned that our Europa rover, the SEV, had been tested right here on the Atacama flats. This landscape, of brown and red, sand and stone, is as Martian as you'll find on planet Earth. I felt, as I had on Melville Island, a sense of exhilaration. The unbroken emptiness expanded inside me. I wanted to make you see it: look, Little Sylvia: nothing.

But the deeper we penetrated, the more I worried. The Atacama would absorb us, I thought. The sameness is suffocating; it closes around you, as if infinity were only another form of constraint. The dust had already consumed our school bus, its Bosom yellow paint job dimming to Martian orange. We had to stop now and then to brush the windscreen with a dampened undergarment.

Those were, for me, the hardest miles. I had made a dreadful mistake bringing you here, trusting Raoul Chips with my child's future. But then, as we crossed the mountains on a faded copper road, Cerro Paranal appeared in the distance. Its summit had been leveled like a Bosom trucker's haircut. On top I saw the four alien figures of its fixed telescopes, white paper boxes. The Sorcerer had been right; he talked like a fool sometimes, but Raoul was right: we had found it. I think I shouted along with the rest. You woke up and cried.

We took the observatory by stages. Though we had traveled six weeks to reach it, Raoul stopped the bus at the base of the hill. He cautioned us against rushing things, but I could see he was scared. Scared that it was a ruin like all the rest.

He chose to send a small recon party up to the base camp. I leapt at the chance to get out in the open air. The futons were moldy with sex and Mexy soft drinks, Raoul's breath was oppressively sour—it had been one long, filthy ride. I dragged a pair of jeans over my paper briefs, pocketed two M-80s to explode as a signal, slipped the blade in my back pocket, and left you in the care of your mother.

A former groundskeeper named Toker accompanied me up the hill. The road had nearly vanished under drifts of coarse sand, but we followed it to the first terrace. Here we found the windowless buildings we now call base camp, arranged around the imposing white Mirror Maintenance Building. The compound looked so bright and welcoming, it might have been built yesterday, except every door was padlocked tight, in anticipation, I suppose, of Smart Man Tolemy and his wrecking crew.

An ancient three-wheeler leaned against one wall of the Mirror Building. I dipped a finger in the reservoir and it was still tacky with oil. In a compartment under the seat, a cheese sandwich was dried crisp but intact.

Toker said something didn't feel right. He said we weren't alone here. "Let's go, man." But I wasn't ready.

Behind the building we made an unexpected discovery. Under a tangled volleyball net lay a wooden hutch, the sort you might see on a Caroline weed farm. The nail heads gleamed. The boards were dry but undamaged. With my blade I pried open the hatch and peered inside. Three white hens roosted on straw.

Toker had seen enough: "Somebody's still here, Rowan. Let's get."

I thought I'd play a little joke on my friend, so I said okay, "but grab us a chicken for the road." Toker had been a farm boy and knew how to approach fowl without spooking them. He crept in soft, hands where those ladies could see them. But when he clapped them around a fat bird, it was like he had popped a piñata, and what was inside wasn't candy.

Toker fell out of the coop holding two fistfuls of dry chicken guts. Bone powder whitened his hair. He doubled over, hacked and wheezed till he coughed up a feather. Inside the hutch, a single egg glowed on the empty nest. Nothing goes away; a desert this dry will not allow it.

I lit an M-80 and hucked it in the air so Raoul could see. That mummy hen was an excellent sign. If vandals had been here long ago to strip the gold and glass from the instruments, they surely would have stopped to eat those birds as well.

Me and Toker watched the bus creep up the road. Everyone got out but Raoul, who gripped the steering wheel and gazed at the hilltop. Someone muttered, "Moses Washington," and I wondered if he would get out at all. Then a smile tore at his face, the wildest look, and Raoul leapt from the door well to roll in the dust with the rest of us.

While Penny sat on the three-wheeler and fired up a weed, I wrapped you in a windbreaker and turned you loose on your new home.

The sun was fixing to set, so we dug in at base camp till dark. The array was still several hundred yards above us, but we wanted to see it as the Astronomers intended, by night. So we waited. We built a fire from the boards of the chicken coop and celebrated with a jumbo tin of potted koi.

Night came. Again it was me and Toker out front, but this time I carried you along in your car seat. When we reached the observation platform at the top of the hill, the Night Glass was no longer above us. It was all around and we were inside it. The Astronomers rightly called our galaxy a Milky Way, for you could feel starlight poured sticky in your hair. The darkness was so absolute that the Earth shrank underfoot to the size of a tetherball, a wobbly thing you had to balance on. I unbuckled your straps and let you waddle across the platform. You whirled among the white domes. Gathered fistfuls of gravel and tossed them at the sky as if all it needed was more stars.

I had already claimed my instrument, a telescope called Kueyen, after a Chilly moon god. Raoul told me she was powerful enough to find a parking spot on Pluto. I circled its openwork dome now, inhaling a faint odor of lubricant, a quickening plastic smell I recalled from the scramble floor of Airplane Food.

Toker hacksawed a U-bolt and opened the doors of the Control Room. A long white building with banks of monitors, carpeted dividers, peeling laminate desks, corkboards and rolling chairs, it reminded me so much of Cape Cannibal's Launch Control that I felt an urge to run. A mug sat on a desk beside a gooseneck lamp. When I stuck in my nose I didn't smell coffee, but I thought of Terry Nguyen on Melville Island and of Umma on her salt dome. Nothing goes away.

18.

MORNING WILL COME SOON. THE MOON ON MY SCREEN will soften and fade. It took two years, but in our clumsy, dogged fashion the Copernican League at last persuaded Kueyen and her sisters to open their eyes. We restored the solar power, tuned up the motors that control the dome movement, booted up the dusty computers, and learned to find a distant target in the dark sky.

Raoul went back to the Residencia an hour ago, leaving us alone in the Control Room. He's getting too old to pull all-nighters. Moving to the sofa, I sit at your grubby feet, one of which pokes through a hole in your sleepsack, counting piggies until you wake up. Always such a heavy sleeper, Little Sylvia.

What might your dreams contain? I haven't provided you with much material. The desert is all you see, nothing but basic geometry colored in without much imagination. A rectangular red plain, the white triangles of distant peaks, the gray ellipse of the distant Pacific. You do not have permission to go to Antafogosta, the ugly village on the bay where we buy our food and toiletries, water by the barrel. You have never seen or heard an animal larger than a beetle. The only birdsong around here is Uncle Raoul's whistled impression of a bob-white. Toker swears he saw a fox, but nobody believes Toker. When I ask you to draw a tree I get a tangle of white limbs full of virus monkeys wearing caps. Gray caps, brown caps, blue caps, red caps. Something from a picture book left behind in our Mexy school bus.

Your birthday is not until tomorrow, but I have an early gift to give you. I carry you to my console and settle you on my knee in your sleepsack. Look here, I say, on the screen. Banded in blue and white and tan like a marbled rubber super-ball, another world. In *The Lonesome Wanderer*, Tolemy made Jupiter the hot-air balloon of the gods, and he was not too far off. Jupiter is our grandest planet, yet made of almost nothing. Only hot vapors with a stone hidden at its core.

A thousand years ago it was a stupid age like our own, run by Jesus Lovers as bully and blind as Chiefs. They said we were special because their Jesus had put the Earth under a dome of painted stars. He'd made a show all for us, and that was the universe.

The eye is a dim and fearful organ, but it was all we had for seeing. Until one early morning like this when the old Astronomer looked through his glass and caught a discomfit-ing sight: moons, strung from the side of Jupiter like bright beads. That, he said, is no wandering star but a world more abundant than our own. Earth is not the center but a suburb, a Hiya City to the great Miamy of the Sun.

It is good to be small, to be one of many. But arrogance is a tumor that by and by grows back. When the Chiefs arrived, they raised a Night Glass above the Earth, they hauled away the telescopes for scrap and left us with our scared little eyes in the dark to feel special and alone.

Lean closer, Little Sylvia, and I will show you what that old Astronomer saw. Here at the edge of the screen: Along come his moons: Ganymede, Callisto, Io, and most precious of all, Europa, like a delicate egg. Inside its shell an embro ready and writhing. Let me pull her close so you can feel where she cracks, here and there, rust brown and gray fissures, fountains of saltwater where the waiting thing scratches to get free.

Through serious child eyes, sticky with sleep, you watch the disc on the screen, trace its circumference with a damp finger, which you jab back in your mouth. This is why I brought you here to the bottom of the world, and now it is my gift to you.

* * *

Faron and Sylvia did the tricky parts. My brother stole not only the Bushmaster rifle from Bill Reade's trailer but also the aykay belonging to Nguyen's goons. I thought Sylvia should not subdue her own parents, but she wouldn't have it any other way. I watched as she stuffed a tube sock into Bill's complaining mouth and suffered a bit thumb for her efforts.

Our own father did not need tying up, but we were careful about what he knew. Faron waited till after midnight to tell him the plan. Pop sat upright, just as he had the previous night, against the headboard watching his toes wriggle under the top sheet. I believe it was a puppet show, two vague figures talking and stroking each other in the dark.

"You ought to run, Pop," Faron whispered. "You might even make it."

Pop listened with a weak smile. It was sound advice that he would not be taking. He only wanted to go back to prison, to Umma by way of the Cuba Pens.

Hours before sunup we exited through the bathroom window, a precaution that was hardly necessary. Our guards slept heavy, one on the picnic table and the other snug in his rubber raft. I don't think they'd even missed their gun.

We said our good-byes under the runty palmetto. What we were doing was right; on this we all agreed. Though I still had questions, chief among them, "How will I know when you get there?"

Faron grinned. He held on to me. "Easy, chief," he said. "In eight years you're going to look up at the sky. When we land we'll give you a signal."

* * *

Launch Control was dark but I did not dare to open the louvered curtain. I knew by feel the location of the power strip. Still, I jumped at the rattle of the old computers as they booted up. The monitors flickered gray, then black, gray again, until the desktops showed a kitten clinging by its front paws to a hopeful blue insignia: HANG IN THERE, NASA!

I tapped the space bar, a sound like a snapped twig that sent grids unfurling down two screens. Numbers filled the cells, all zeroes. Three smaller screens provided video. On one I saw the Space Launch System cling to its tower; another looked inside the White Room, a platform at the top of the tower where Faron and Sylvia would stand for the last time before leaving Earth. I watched them enter, suit up, and exit right to reappear on the final screen inside the cockpit. Faron looked toward the camera and, though he could not see my face, offered two vigorous birdie fingers and a grin.

Once I initiated the sequence, the compressors would commence their noisy work, steam would shriek from the vents, the ground would quake. Terry Nguyen, woken by the noise, would have exactly four minutes to scramble his goons and abort the liftoff.

I typed a password, which was *snowballschance*, and watched the numbers rise and fall inside the grids. At the bottom of each screen a cursor blinked. I would have to type two numerical codes simultaneously, one on each keyboard.

I typed 811118. I typed 922229.

The final prompt appeared: PRESS ESC TO INITIATE LAUNCH SEQUENCE.

"We're inside," said Faron. "Restart the clock."

I touched the two escape keys and drew a breath that I would not exhale for many seconds. Outside I heard a loud rush, as of rain through a busted downspout. High on the wall the countdown clock flashed once, then went black. A pause. When the digits reappeared days and hours had vanished, all the months of terror and misgiving that began in that ruined zoo—erased. Everything, I thought, was about to start over.

00:00:04:00, read the clock.

"Wait!" said Sylvia.

"What?" I said.

"You said you'd tell us," said Sylvia.

"I did," I said. "I did tell."

"I thought there would be another step. I thought you'd say something else." I had not heard her like this before, that hard voice broken by fright.

"What's happening?" she said. "Is it supposed to shake like this?"

Now I jabbed at the escape keys, retyped the numbers, the password, yanked the keyboard from the wall. I wanted to stop time, just for a moment, so that we could all catch our breath.

Then came my brother's voice, calm: "Rowan. It's too late. We're already gone."

The clock read 00:00:03:34.

"Is this right?" I shouted. "Is this what ought to happen?"

Sylvia's voice returned, shaking from what might have been fear or only the vibrations. "You're doing good." But I knew she was only trying to make me feel right. Light spilled through the gaps in the steel blinds.

When I opened them I saw the mound of launchpad 39B set ablaze. Smoke piped out of the flame trench, higher than the tower, giant, ghost, genie. I watched the rigging tremble; I watched the air tremble. And for the first time that morning I felt certain: they were going to Europa; I was helping.

When the clock ran down to two minutes, I returned to check the monitors. Sylvia and Faron were strapped in. My brother showed his tongue in a dirty laugh, but Sylvia just stared. I stared back knowing she could not see me. I should have said something, but nothing came; any words would have been too small. I have endured lonely mornings since, but when I looked into Sylvia's face on the little gray screen, that was the most sorrowful of all. Everyone was leaving.

* * *

"It's your uncle lives there on Europa. Him and your pretty Aunt Sylvia."

"Sylvia," you say, made happy by the coincidence.

* * *

At one minute, twenty-six seconds to liftoff, I walked out of the control room carrying the Bushmaster. I leapt down whole flights of stairs till I reached the bottom, but as I rounded the hall to enter the lobby, I stopped.

"Don't shoot us!" It was the Bosom goons. They looked more frightened of me than I was of them. I had a gun. I don't recall leveling it at those men or if I even bothered to switch off the safety. Anyway, their hands were in the air.

I backed toward the entrance, where a blue tarp hung over the busted frame. To my left I saw the men's room. Bill's instructions were to force the guards inside and padlock the door behind them, but I'd forgotten the lock and had no experience forcing anyone to do anything. I recall making a vague gesture toward the toilet. They looked at me, confused now as well as scared.

"Kid," said the one who liked word-search puzzles, "we're not going to do nothing. If this is when you need to run, go for it."

I sprinted across the parking lot until I hit a stand of scrub palms, where I followed the indolent little creek to our trailers. There I heard Bill Reade howling. I pictured his sock popping free like a cork, and almost smiled at his stupid rage. Then I heard what he was shouting: Terry Nguyen's name. He was in the Reades' trailer and Bill was begging him not to do something. He said it was me, all me.

In my panic I tripped over Pop's brogans and realized I was lying atop Umma's grave. Before running on, I slipped the rifle into the water. Deep in the mangrove the noise grew intolerable. I pressed my palms to my ears and watched as the gantry arms swung free. The rocket pushed up on its pillar of steam; sheets of ice slid off the booster.

Inside Orion the pressure would be cellular; flesh and bone, organ meats, eyes, nerves, and tubing, every bit of their bodies clinging to the Earth where they had been made. Sylvia and Faron could see nothing but approaching sky, an eternity or else a sudden stop. Sylvia might tell herself she no longer believed in the Night Glass, but a fear so carefully built is not easily broken. Eight minutes after liftoff, though, when the gray arc of the upper atmosphere showed through the window, as the black spread out to describe the whole of the Earth, the planets and distant stars, they would believe. They had left sorrow and solitude miles below. Ahead lay Europa.

I stood on Old Cape Road as the sun mounted the sea and realized I had nowhere to go.

* * *

Now, after eight years' travel, as we watch from distant Chilly, they prepare to land. Here is what they do: They check the couplings to the Habitat, the SEV, and the Penguin, strap themselves into the Lander, and initiate de-orbit. They land beside a thermal vent on the surface of Europa, disengage the Penguin and the Habitat. They check the water spinach in its substrate, feed the rabbits, fix themselves a mug of tea. Eight years it took them to reach Europa. Eight years before I knew where I was heading. Here, with you, Little Sylvia, waiting for a signal.

19.

THIS MORNING COMES AS A SURPRISE. MOST DAYS THE sun rolls up slowly, a blue glow behind the Andes. It teases between the distant peaks, a game of galactic cat-and-mouse. My work requires total darkness, and though I am exhausted by sunup, I'm always sad to see the day come. But today it sneaks up behind me, taps me brightly on the shoulder. Imagine: me, an Astronomer surprised by the sun.

Down the white steps I carry you outside the Control Room. In the glare of the platform you strain to open your eyes. I stand you on your sleeping-bagged feet and your head falls sleepily against my leg. Then you remember, and your eyes spring open. You are now three, and your wish is to spend the day with your father, playing among the buildings of base camp, your favorite place in this abbreviated world.

"Hop!" I say. "Hop, birthday bunny!" Another sight I have deprived you of, the rabbit with its buttered fur, its lean, rich meat and preposterous ears. We could raise them here, I think, if we rebuilt the chicken coop. We will need something to barter when the money gives out. I should talk to Penny.

Below the observatory platform, the entrance to the Residencia peeks out from the slope. The road is the easiest way to reach it, but you insist we take the Star Track, a switchback trail the Astronomers used for long contemplative hikes. The stones along the path are etched with alien images, of stretch-neck horses like they kept at Zoo Miamy, of human figures with multiple eyes and radiating heads, chiseled gray astronauts. You call them your "rock guys." They wave hello from the past, hello to Little Sylvia. You always wave back.

I turn one over to show you its damp underside, where lichen whitens the stone. A tiny insect hurries into a shadow. Life insists, even here. Our first summer in the Atacama—you would not remember—a rainstorm blew in from Bolivay and the most remarkable thing happened: flowers. By the millions. One face of Cerro Paranal broke out in a rash of toy lilies and delicate blue poppies. Raoul thought it was obscene, a desecration. I made sure you danced among them, gathered a bouquet to give to grumpy Uncle Chips. In a week the flowers had returned to the sand to wait for rain's return.

The Star Track is pitched and slippery. You make a big show of whipping your arms back till you slide downhill on your corduroys. I chase after shouting; you must be more careful. You are all I have. But you just laugh at the minor avalanche you have caused.

In the lobby of the Residencia we find Raoul posted at his usual spot, legs dangling in the empty plunge pool, not sipping his coffee. Chilly has little in the way of food, but coffee is plentiful. Penny roasts it in a former lima bean can with an acetylene torch. I haven't developed a taste for the stuff, but I wouldn't make it through the long nights without a thermosful. It is no coincidence that Astronomy vanished with coffee.

The Residencia has twenty suites, each with a cramped bed, a miniature desk, and a washing-machine window. Less elbow room than the Gables, perhaps, but at least you don't get shanked on the stairs.

Nobody gets much sleep in the desert. It's the quiet wakes you up. No crickets, no traffic, no weather. Only the watery rush of the cryostat to assure you that you haven't gone deaf. The air is so dry, you can hardly breathe. We dream of dust, in our throats, in our eyes, and wake up choking.

When the Gunts stopped sending money, and food or medicine could not be had in Atofogasta, the caretakers simply drifted away, leaving piles of journals, a crate of whiskey, and a closetful of board games that are now yours. One woman must have refused to leave. We found her desiccated corpse stretched out on the chaise longue beside the pool, a heavier sleeper than you. She had wrapped herself in duvets so that only her face showed in the folds. She had made her own shroud and lay down to wait.

Penny declared her pretty, though I could not see the appeal. The skin had gone stiff as Pop's wallet. The woman's name had been Lieben, Jennifer, and from her journals I gather that she studied the formation of gas giants around distant stars of a certain magnitude. There was great concern in those dying days for how things began.

She wore on one mummy middle finger a ring set with a milky white stone. It had taken some effort to remove it, but for your second birthday I strung the ring on a piece of twine for you to wear around your neck.

This year, I gave you a moon, milky white.

Raoul likes to joke that he will die like Jennifer Lieben, dried up beside an empty pool. You hug him good morning, he wishes you another fine birthday, calls you his monkey, and then stiffly climbs the stairs to his bed. I fill two cups of coffee, one for me and one for you, with extra powdered goat milk. Our habits here are not numerous but they are ironclad. We sip and walk carefully the final stretch down to the base camp.

The buildings have been a trove of relics. A book of pressed flowers, photos, an entire housecat taxidermied by the desert. I once found a jelly donut so hard, I used it to drive a nail through plywood. We call base camp Sylvia's Toy Store. But you already have the best birthday present I can give, Europa, where Sylvia and Faron will one day send us a sign, and we will be a family again.

I say run. Three times around the Mirror Building, one for every precious year you have lived. I time you, counting one one thousand, two one thousand . . .

When you finish your final orbit, I catch you, damp and out of breath, in my arms, and tell you what I know.

"Have many happy birthdays, Little Sylvia. May you die before you are alone."

Thanks to my hunter college teachers and friends, especially Jason Porter, who kindly read this story when it was still a lump. Thanks to Dr. Franck Marchis, of SETI, and Dr. Mike Wong, of UC Berkeley, for preventing certain embarrassment about matters astronomical. This novel would not have crept out of the primordial ooze had my agent, Nicole Aragi, not coaxed it forth with patience and encouragement. Thanks to So Caroline's own Duvall Osteen for keeping the machine flapping smoothly. My unparalleled (seriously) editor, Riva Hocherman, improved this book in ways I could not have imagined. Thanks to my family for their steady support. For reading every word and giving her unerringly good advice, thanks to Margaret. For knowing that I'd misspelled *Ptolemy*, thanks to Felix.

About the Author

JEFFREY ROTTER is the author of *The Unknown Knowns* and *The Only Words That Are Worth Remembering*. His fiction and nonfiction have appeared in *The New York Times*, the *Oxford American*, the *Boston Review*, and elsewhere. He grew up in Columbia, South Carolina, and is a longtime resident of Brooklyn, New York, where he lives with his wife and son.